#accidentmurderer

Quineka Ragsdale

To those without a voice, your story will still be told.

CHAPTERS

1 FRANKLIN MARTIN

"But check this – " Frank stopped in the middle of his sentence. He straightened up his seat and turned towards the front of the classroom, expecting to see his teacher walk in.

"Where's Coach?" Coach Black poked his head in their classroom, looking to Frank for an answer.

Frank knew he only asked him because he sat right by the door. "I don't know." Frank shrugged. "Maybe he's late."

Coach Black's head disappeared. He closed the door just as quickly as he had opened it. Frank took that as his cue to continue his one-man show for the class.

"On the cool though, Coach Bobby shouldn't have provoked him like that. He know Brodrick can fight," Frank said. "How many players has he whooped after the game?"

"Brodrick hasn't had a fight after the game in years. I don't even think Coach was here then," Lisa added.

"Yea, but Coach is like six foot-three, 200 pounds. You'd think he could hold his own," Kenny scoffed. "Didn't he say he could bench his weight?"

"That ain't got shit to do with fighting," Frank blurted as he stood.

They were used to Coach Bobby coming in late after lunch, but the bell rung over thirty minutes ago. Frank figured he called in sick after being beaten bloody by the leading scorer. That or he was embarrassed.

Loosening his tie, Frank stood at the front of the room to reenact the fight.

"You're messing with my future." Frank mimicked the last words that grabbed his attention before watching the repeated blows the coach received from his star player.

Frank swiveled his head left and right, wincing for effect. He clutched his stomach, pretending to be hurt while slowly falling backward over Coach Bobby's desk. Most of the students laughed at either his comical acting skills or the fate that their history teacher had endured.

The incident happened the day before, during basketball practice. Less than a handful of the students in class were there to witness. They needed each basketball player to retell the story of Brodrick beating down Coach Bobby. All the students loved Coach Bobby, but they also loved Brodrick. Although Franklin knew it wasn't a funny story, he had to make light of such a dramatic event.

"That's not even how it happened," Justin called from the left of the room.

"Okay, well you be Coach Bobby and I'll be Brodrick," Frank responded.

"Naw, Frank. I really don't think it's funny."

"Then what happened then," the kid with the Coke bottle glasses said to Justin. Frank didn't take the kid for a gossiper, but he asked the question the other students wore on their faces.

Justin glanced over the half-dozen inquiring faces staring at him. The room grew quiet as a half-dozen more turned to face him as well.

"Well…" Frank urged. Since Justin was so adamant about interrupting his story, he must have had something to add.

"Coach was caught off guard is all I'm saying. Had he known B was gone do that, he would have been ready."

Everyone turned their faces back to the front of the room, awaiting a response from Frank.

"Y'all know my mixtape comes out Friday, right? Think I might add a little freestyle about the basketball fight of the century." Frank glanced at the imaginary sign he cleared in the sky as he spoke.

"He didn't get caught off guard. He probably provoked him." Kenny stole Frank's attention. The class now looked in his direction. "He's always saying inappropriate stuff about Chemere."

"Maybe that's what he meant about Coach messing with his future, huh?" Frank instigated. He caught Josephina rolling her eyes. "Kenny, you be Brodrick, I'll be Coach." Frank desperately tried to reclaim the attention of his classmates.

Again, Frank moved his head from left to right while backing into the desk.

Kenny laughed, "I can't fight in a suit, man. My mama will kill me if I tear this thing." Kenny straightened his suit jacket as he talked. "This the only suit I got."

Franklin loosened his tie again at the mention of a suit. He hated that the basketball team had to wear suits on game days. Another stupid change Coach Bobby made for the team. He said it made them look more respectable. *This is high school,* Frank thought, *I have the rest of my life to look respectable.*

"Alright, alright. I guess I'll have to do this reenactment myself."

"You keep on boy, Coach Bobby gone walk in right while you're falling over on his desk." Lisa giggled.

"After that ass whooping yesterday? I doubt it. He probably called in sick from embarrassment. Okay, this what happened."

Frank took it upon himself to tell the class the same story they heard about since the evening before. Practice was about to begin when Brodrick and Coach Bobby were talking by the bleachers. Since the beginning of the season, it wasn't unusual for them to have a disagreement. Therefore, the few players that tossed the basketball around didn't stop to listen.

Frank was on the court shooting and passing the basketball to Justin and Kenny. Rogue was stretching on the other end of the bleachers while talking to Coach Black. Frank had just knocked the ball out of Justin's grasp when it rolled near the entrance. Mike walked into the gym with some tall, super black, lanky dude. The lanky kid picked up the ball to return it to Frank's awaiting hands when he froze in his tracks. *You're messing with my future* echoed in the gym. Frank turned to the sound of Brodrick's yell to see where the lanky kid stared.

Coach Bobby was already a bloody pulp, kissing the gym floor. Everything, from his hands to his pockets, was sprawled all over the floor as Coach Bobby cowered to Brodrick's wrath.

The entire team, even those who only seconds before dressed in the locker room, were now surrounding Brodrick and Coach Bobby. Kenny and Mike pulled Brodrick away from their coach while Coach Black and Justin helped lift coach from the ground. Frank, the lanky kid, and Rogue began gathering coach's things that lie across the floor. When Frank saw that Brodrick was about to escape Kenny and Mike's grasp, he dropped the clipboard he held to help remove him from the gym.

Everything happened so quickly that Frank wasn't sure how the fight got started. But because he was there, he felt he was responsible for retelling the story. The rest of the school needed to know what an epic event they had missed. Hamer High was a pretty uneventful school. They hardly had fights, never any bomb threats, and even the protests were coordinated with both the students and the staff. This was the most exciting thing that happened in Frank's four years at Hamer, and he was going to revel in every moment of it.

Frank finally got to his favorite part. The part where he dramatically exclaimed Brodrick's echoing words while sustaining invisible blow after blow. The final blow knocked him over Coach Bobby's desk. His classmates' laughter grew louder and louder until he heard a loud thud.

In a split second, the laughter turned into long oohs, for which Frank knew he was to blame. His feet found balance as his eyes met the paperweight that fell to the floor. The marble paperweight was shaped like a life-sized apple. Frank wrapped his palm around the name *Rob*, which was engraved in the center of the apple. He quickly placed the apple on the edge of the desk and turned to return to his seat. The classroom door opened.

Ms. Johnson stood in his path, staring him squarely in the eyes. He didn't remember her being so tall. He lowered his head in shame, noticing her six-inch heels. "Are we being a class clown again, Mr. Martin?"

Frank hated when people used *we* when he knew they meant *you*. He also hated rhetorical questions. They served no real purpose. He used to have a crush on Ms. Johnson, but she always talked to him like she was somebody's mama.

"I was simply picking up that apple that somehow fell on the floor." Frank took his seat to the right of Coach Bobby's desk. He made sure not to make eye contact with her.

"Respect the classroom. I can hear y'all all the way in the hall."

Frank heard Ms. Johnson's phone buzz as she took it from her jacket pocket. She stared at her phone while scrolling as she spoke to no one in particular. "I'm sure Coach Bobby will be here soon."

"We haven't seen him all day, Miss," Frank heard Lisa say. He turned to look at his classmates. Most of them were busy writing or looking at their books. Frank chuckled. If he didn't know any better, he'd swear they were working the whole time they were in class. Justin caught his eye.

"Frank said he'd teach the class about his mixtape," Justin said loud enough for Ms. Johnson to hear. Justin was a hater for no reason. That's why Frank always gave him a hard time.

Frank turned to face Ms. Johnson, preparing to rebut her response. Her facial expression stunned him. Frantically typing on her phone, her mouth was gaped open while her eyes were lost in sorrow. When she finished tapping her phone, she glanced away. Her eyes slowly trailed to Coach Bobby's desk. "Oh my God. Bobby is dead?"

Frank wasn't sure he had heard her right. She spoke barely above a whisper. "What was that, Ms. Johnson? What did you say?"

Her face was still in shock. The buzzing of her phone startled her. She began tapping on it again.

"Did you say Coach Bobby was dead?" Frank asked.

"What?"

"Huh?"

"Are you serious?"

Frank could hear his classmates' questions behind him. Ms. Johnson finally looked up at the class. She looked like she wanted to say something, but nothing came out of her mouth.

"Did you say Coach Bobby was dead?" Frank asked her again. She looked at him or maybe she looked through him. Frank couldn't tell.

The bell rang. The students raced each other out of the door while Ms. Johnson looked around in shock. Frank lingered in front of her for a moment, but realized she wasn't going to give him any answers. In a boring school, information traveled fast. He'd find the answers elsewhere.

His next class was full of quiet rumors, but their teacher, Mr. Jackson, wouldn't allow discussion about anything that had nothing to do with Calculus. He took joy in collecting students' phones if they even looked like they wanted to use them. Frank didn't get confirmation of Coach Bobby's death until he was on the way to his car after school.

A pale, skinny lady in plastic red frames quickly moved her short legs to follow a student who looked like the Michelin man. Michelin man roughly shook his head several times before she gave up. He watched as she sped toward the super black, lanky dude who did a quick about-face in her presence. His obvious avoidance didn't slow her stride. She quickly made eye contact with Frank.

Frank took one second too long noticing that her crisp button-down top, pencil skirt, stockings and short heels looked out of place. That one second was all she needed to have his attention. Long enough to ask him a startling question.

"Can you tell me what you know about your star basketball player killing his coach?"

2 NATALIA RANDLE

Natalia was excited. She finally had a good story to write. Either her editor didn't see her skills or he had no faith in her. He never gave her important stories to cover. She was hanging out with a friend, complaining about her editor's insistence on her covering high school basketball games.

"I have to cover the Hamer vs Moors basketball game tomorrow," she sighed with angst. "I didn't even watch high school basketball when I was in high school. I've told my editor over and over, but he's not listening."

"Fannie Lou Hamer High school?" her friend asked. "We just booked one of their basketball players before I left work. I think they said he assaulted his coach."

Natalia spit out the juice she was drinking. "What? The coach of his basketball team? Where did this happen?"

"It was at the school. At practice, I think. He was this tall, angry kid. Very intimidating. He still had on his practice jersey," her friend confirmed.

A huge smile spread across Natalia's face. The boring story she hated could likely turn into the story she needed to propel her career. She found out everything she could before leaving dinner abruptly.

It took all night, but Natalia got another friend to leak copies of the police report that Coach Bobby filed. She quickly snapped photos of the file with her phone before her friend changed his mind.

Natalia stopped by the office first thing the next morning to tell her boss the exciting news. He was in a meeting when she got there, so she decided to read over notes at her desk.

She knew that Brodrick Timmons was the promising NBA prospect from Hamer's basketball team, but she didn't understand why he would assault his coach. She had seen the photos. Coach Bobby's right eye and his lip were swollen. He looked pretty bad. It might take days before she could get an interview with Brodrick, but Coach Bobby was just a drive away.

She dialed the number to Fannie Lou Hamer High School. She had talked with Coach Bobby a few times before, to get quotes on his winning streak and how he had turned the team around. She suspected that he would be okay with talking to her. She wouldn't mention anything about the assault until she could see him in person.

"Hello." Natalia recognized the office manager's voice.

"Hi, Ms. Dewberry. How are you doing today?"

"I won't complain. How may I help you?" Ms. Dewberry's curt demeanor never offended Natalia. She was a busy lady.

"This is Natalia Randle from the Elite Telegram. I'm calling for Coach Bobby."

"Hold, please."

Natalia put the phone on speaker. Ms. Dewberry was never in a hurry to return to the phone.

Natalia looked up to see the conference room door opening. Her boss was just exiting his meeting. Out of the five men who left the conference room, he and the lead writer, Tim, were the only two laughing. Natalia felt her face turn into a scowl. He'd probably give her story to Tim if she told him. She knew that no one had caught wind of the story yet. She wanted the story to run in the next day's paper. She decided to wait until press deadline to tell her boss.

"Hello. Natalia?"

She grabbed the receiver quickly. "Yes, Ms. Dewberry. I'm here."

"Coach Bobby isn't here today."

"Do you know if he'll come in later?"

"No clue. You can try back later if you want."

"Ok. Thanks." Natalia hung up the phone and power walked to her car.

She had Coach Bobby's home address on one of the photos she had taken. She quickly typed the address on Clydesdale Street into her phone's GPS before pulling out of the parking lot.

She fantasized about adding the title *This is a Natalia Randle Exclusive* to the news story. She had a friend who was doing very well with an exposé blog, *Underground News*. He'd learn of all kinds of dirt from local politicians and local personalities. He had a way of getting facts from people without revealing his sources. She could do that. Nah. She quickly erased those thoughts. Her dream was to make true journalism popular again. No more gossip or yellow journalism. Just hardcore facts so the readers could make well-informed decisions rather than biased opinions based on emotions.

Natalia pulled up to Coach Bobby's house behind a big white van. She grabbed her recorder and hopped out of the car. Before reaching the sidewalk, Natalia realized that something was wrong. There were two police cars parked in front of the van. She looked at the van. Through the broad, blue stripe, it read *Coroner.*

Two men hopped out of the van wearing long black jumpsuits with matching boots. Natalia didn't know why, but her heart started pounding. Something bad had happened there.

"Ma'am, is this your car?" One of the men in the jumpsuit asked.

Natalia nodded.

"We need to get the gurney out the back. Can you please back up your vehicle?"

Natalia caught her composure. "Of course."

Natalia moved her car, allowing a few dozen feet between her and the van. She decided instead of hopping out so fast, she could likely gain a lot from simply watching.

There was a man standing at Coach Bobby's door. He was wiping his eyes while talking with two police officers. One officer placed his hand on the man's shoulder to console him. The men moved away from the door once the gurney came near. This act caused the man to turn and weep. Natalia recognized the man talking with the officers. It was Coach Black. He was Coach Bobby's assistant coach. This must have meant that Coach Bobby was dead.

Natalia felt a rush of energy. Confused feelings jumbled inside of her. This would be a great opportunity to ask a mentor for help. Although he passed her on many opportunities, she knew that her boss would know what to do.

At the thought of her boss, she realized this is probably why he thought she didn't have the necessary skills to cover top stories. Here she was, on the brink of a breaking news story and she was scared. In her Journalism classes, she didn't learn how to interview loved ones of the recently deceased.

She knew that the human thing to do would be to give Coach Black time. To allow the police space to do their job. But if she did that, Tim would be there getting her scoop. She had to find some courage, some drive or something to get the story first.

Natalia hopped out of the car just when the coroners were bringing the gurney back down the sidewalk. Underneath the long, dark body bag, she could tell there was a person. A man who seemed as tall as Coach Bobby. A man whose shoulders seemed as wide as Coach Bobby's.

Natalia heaved. She liked Coach Bobby. He was such a charming man. He was tall and very attractive. He had dark eyebrows and a perfectly trimmed mustache with a small beard that framed his chestnut brown face. Every time she interviewed him, she felt like she was the only person in the room. She often thought his eyes twinkled as he told her the joys of his basketball game.

Natalia had to put her feelings behind her. "Is that Coach Bobby?" she blurted. The voice sounded weary. It was small and very unsure.

One of the men opened the back door of the van. They both looked to one another before resting their eyes on Natalia.

Natalia straightened her posture. She smoothed the wrinkles in her face before speaking again. "Is that Robert Charles Maker?" Natalia questioned with Coach Bobby's full name she remembered from the police report. She was proud that her voice was now more assertive. She felt that it commanded their attention.

"You may want to talk to the officers, ma'am," one of the men responded. They proceeded to put the body into the back of the van.

Natalia followed the driver to his side of the van. "Please, sir. Off the record. My name is Natalia Randle from *The Elite Telegram*." She pulled her retractable badge from her waist to show him.

The man looked to the left and right of him before acknowledging her. "Off the record?" he asked.

"Yes. Is this the basketball coach from Hamer High School?"

"I think that's what I overheard the officers say, but I don't know anything else." The man jumped in the van and slammed the door. Natalia walked away once the ignition started.

She walked around the van before it drove off. A police officer ushered Coach Black to his car. He nodded a few times before finally getting in. Natalia watched the officers leave. She took a deep breath then approached Coach Black, who was still sitting in his car.

With his eyes focused in his lap, he typed on his phone while tears flowed from his face. Natalia hated to approach him, but she needed the scoop. Although she still thought it was a bit insensitive, she decided to practice her friend's technique. Using the blunt element of surprise to learn the hard, cold facts she needed to build a story.

"Excuse me, Coach Black." She stood by his door until he acknowledged her.

His bloodshot eyes were confused. He turned on the car and rolled down his window.

"Coach Black," Natalia started. "I know this is a difficult time, but I'd like to get a statement from you on Coach Bobby's death."

A new set of tears began to stream from his eyes. His shoulders shook in an upheaval rant.

"I was going to ask about tonight's game, but it looks like his death came all of a sudden. Do you know if this has anything to do with Brodrick's assault?" Natalia tried her best to sound apologetic, but she had to ask the right questions. She held her recorder in hand, awaiting his response.

"I tried to get him to go to the hospital. I told him to let them check him out. He just didn't listen. If only he listened. I can't…" Coach Black raised the window as he sobbed. The interview was over.

Natalia didn't waste a moment. She mouthed *I'm sorry* to Coach Black and drove straight to Fannie Lou Hamer High. She knew school wasn't over for a couple more hours, but she'd make sure she was first on the scene.

Natalia parked across the street from the school. She decided against interviewing the administration first. She knew the staff would have to be politically correct in their responses. They may not even know that he had died. It seemed that Coach Black had just learned of Coach Bobby's death himself.

She'd speak to the students first. Maybe she could catch someone from the basketball team. Teenagers wouldn't try to be politically correct. As a matter of fact, most of them would love their fifteen seconds of fame. She pulled out her laptop to frame her story.

Moments before the bell rang, she hopped out of the car with her recorder in hand.

The first student that came out of the school wore a white T-shirt and white jeans. The food stains on his shirt alluded that he never missed lunch. He had to be at least three times her size. Although she knew he wasn't on the basketball team, she figured he could have known Coach Bobby. Most of the upperclassmen took his history class and the teen could easily be an upperclassman.

It didn't matter if the kid was an upperclassman or not. He declined to speak with Natalia without even hearing what she had to say. Teens were mean.

Natalia didn't let that get her down. He was the first kid to come out, but hundreds would follow. She then saw a dark brown, almost purple-colored giant kid burst through the doors. She didn't remember him being on the basketball team, but he had to have been a player. She got her tape recorder together and made a B-line toward him.

"Excuse me. Do you-" The kid amazon made an instant pivot and walked in the same direction he had just come from. Natalia sighed. Teens were weird.

She then noticed a familiar face. One of the players from the basketball team. He was one of the few she remembered because he was always joking. He liked to be seen. She smiled; she'd give him the chance he wanted.

Right after blurting out her question to him, she realized that she sounded insensitive. The teen sighed.

"Look. I just heard that he died. I don't know what to tell you." He looked around at the other students who were rushing away from school.

"Is it Justin?" Natalia asked. "I remember you." She smiled.

He put his hand over his heart and gave her a look of astonishment. His face relaxed into an aha moment. "You heard my mixtape was coming out? I actually go by the name J. Bird."

It took a second for Natalia to hide her confusion. She could use that information to her advantage.

"I'm from *The Elite Telegram*." She showed him her badge. "I usually write about your team's winning streak, but I just learned of Coach Bobby's death. I want to make sure we have something in the paper tomorrow."

Justin looked uninterested.

"I can try to include something about your upcoming mixtape if I get a quote from you. I'll be sending the story to my editor in about an hour. This shouldn't take long."

Justin smiled.

He told her of the outlandish story regarding a fight that left Coach Bobby bruised and bloody. "Yea, I saw the photo from the police report," Natalia told him to keep him talking.

"Man, you got it like that?"

"What I don't understand is why Brodrick hit Coach Bobby in the first place."

"Word on the street is that it had something to do with Brodrick's girl, Chemere."

"They were fighting over a high school girlfriend?" That seemed unbelievable to Natalia. "Well, you were there. Do you think Bobby's injuries were enough to cause his death?"

Justin's hand met his chin. "I didn't think about it like that. Man, Coach was bloody. That was a lot of blood. I wouldn't be surprised. But Coach just went home after the cops took Brodrick. I thought everything was okay, though." He put his hand on his hip. "Coach was gone make sure Brodrick did time. He said he wanted to press charges like ten times. I was like dang, we get it. You want him to go to jail. He's going."

Justin's face wrinkled. "I hope he didn't die of a concussion or something. That would be horrible for Brodrick. I can't believe this is happening. Coach really was a good dude. He could be an asshole sometimes, but he was a really good dude. This is going to be hard on the team."

Natalia could tell that Justin had only now began to realize the severity of the situation. She wanted her next question to be softer, more upbeat.

"But anyway. My mixtape comes out Friday. It's called Sounds of a

Real Dude. It'll be on Soundcloud, Apple Music, Google Play or wherever you like to get your music. It's fire. The game was canceled, so I'm headed to the studio right now. You give me a shout out, I'll give you a shout out."

Natalia frowned. "Um...okay." Teens were not focused.

3 MICHAEL JOHNSON

By now everyone knew that Coach Bobby was dead. School was still going on, but no one was focused. Even the teachers. Especially the teachers. Coach had only been at the school for two years, but he was a favorite amongst students. Being a possible NBA prospect, the basketball team's captain and the leading scorer on the basketball team, Brodrick was easily the most popular student in the school. He was even most popular four years ago when he was just a freshman. The students didn't want to choose sides, but they felt like they needed to. With Brodrick in jail and Coach dead, walking through Hamer was like walking through a graveyard.

"Let me see that," Mike asked Justin for the newspaper article he was reading aloud to the class.

They were in English class and it was basically free time. Their teacher, Mr. Whittington, told them to read or talk amongst themselves, just not to be too loud. Mr. Whittington walked in and out of class, seemingly too busy to teach.

"How did this article come out so fast? We just found out that he died last night," Mike said. "And of all people, why did she talk to Frank?"

Justin passed Mike the newspaper.

"Would you have talked to her if she tried to interview you?"

"Naw," Mike uttered while looking over the article.

He glanced at Brodrick's mugshot and the huge picture of Coach Bobby with the team before reading over the article. Brodrick's scowl reminded him of the old Brodrick.

"And do you see where it says he has that stupid mixtape coming out?" Justin added.

Michael read where the assault happened after practice Monday and where Coach refused to go to the hospital against both Coach Black's and the ambulance driver's suggestion. He also read that an autopsy would be done.

"This doesn't say that it was Brodrick's fault, though." Mike peered over the article.

"Let me see that," the student next to him asked. He passed the paper to the kid with the Coke bottle glasses.

"It says he was assaulted, Brodrick went to jail and now he's dead. That's the same thing, ain't it? Maybe he didn't mean to kill him, but he's dead. Murder by accident. They're calling him an accident murderer." Justin shrugged.

"All because he said something about Chemere?" Nosy Josephina chimed in.

"She didn't even come to school today," Lisa added. "People are blaming her for Coach Bobby's death."

"Dang, for real?" Mike spewed. He had heard about the story trending on social media. Everyone in the city was commenting about it.

"Coach could have any woman he wanted. I doubt they were arguing over her," Justin insisted. "She alright, but she ain't all that."

Mike knew that Justin was just hating, but he didn't feel a need to state the obvious.

"I bet y'all gone miss those bomb ass player parties on Clydesdale street," the kid next to Mike blurted.

Mike side-eyed the kid for a second. His edge-up wasn't even straight and he had powdered donut lips. Again, Mike kept his comments to himself, but snatched the newspaper before turning away.

"Naw," Justin uttered. "That's the least of our worries." Justin sighed. His voice faded lower, "The accident murderer has made us the laughing stock of the city. I can't believe this. I'm gone miss Coach, man."

Mike thought back to the incident. Monday was always a light practice because they had a game the next day. He was in great spirits at the time, too. He was running a few minutes late for practice, but stopped when he saw a new student. The kid stood at eye level with him. The tallest kids in the school were all on the basketball team and only a few members of the basketball team measured up to him. He had never seen this kid before. He was pencil thin and the color of smooth dark pencil led. Mike could tell that the guy was lost.

"Ay. What's up, man?" He approached him.

"Hey. I'm looking for the gym."

"I'm headed that way myself. Are you looking to join the basketball team?" Mike asked.

"I don't know really. I told my mom I'd check it out on the first day."

"What are you," Mike looked him up and down. "About 6' 3"?" Mike thought they were the same height.

The kid straightened his posture. "Actually, I'm 6' 6". Slouching is a bad habit."

"Oh damn." Mike was shocked at his instant growth. "Coach is going to love you. Come on."

Mike escorted the new guy to the gym. He learned that he was from

Florida and hadn't played ball since he was a kid. Mike instantly knew that wasn't going to fly for Coach Bobby, but he didn't say anything.

He must have worn an expression on his face because he said, "I know I'd have to earn a spot on the team. I was thinking I could just start out practicing with the team and maybe just be a water boy or something. I've heard about Hamer going to state every year. I know I can't just walk on."

Mike smirked. He felt embarrassed that he could read his thoughts.

"What made you move to Texas?" Mike changed the subject.

"Oh, we've been here for years. We just moved to this district because my mom got a new job in this area."

"I've been at Hamer all four years. I couldn't imagine having to make new friends and change my whole schedule. But most people are pretty cool. You'll soon find out that the school hangout spot is at Coach's green and yellow house on Clydesdale Street."

"That's good to know, man." The guy smiled. "I'm only a junior so I'll have time to figure some things out. It's good to get a fresh start."

Mike opened the gym door. The new guy walked in first, picking up the basketball that was rolling their way. Mike could hear a voice echo before looking around the new guy to see Coach Bobby fall to the floor. Brodrick had kicked him at least twice before Mike could come to Coach's aid.

Brodrick was extremely angry. Mike had played ball with Brodrick since middle school. They weren't best friends, but they were cool. He had never seen Brodrick that angry. Even when he picked up the nasty habit of fighting the players from the other team, he was never very angry. He'd just laugh it off after the fight was broken up. He didn't even hold a grudge after the fight. They saw those same players year after year, and he'd only say something nasty to them if they had said something mean to him first.

"None of this makes sense," Mike said to his listening classmates. "I doubt that Brodrick would be fighting over his girlfriend. Do you guys really think Coach was interested in Chemere?"

"I'd believe it," Lisa murmured.

Mike caught Justin and Lisa sharing a knowing glance. Justin noticed Mike watching.

"You know how Coach is always joking around. Maybe he just said a joke," Justin stated. "Was anyone paying attention to them before the fight broke out?"

"I was too busy showing the new guy the gym." Mike shook his head.

"Well, we saw what Brodrick did to Coach," Justin expressed.

"That doesn't mean he's the one who killed him," Lisa said. "He could have died of anything."

"Like what, Lisa? Coach was a certified athlete," Justin expressed.

"He didn't even eat red meat. He was healthy as a horse."

"Let's hope, for Brodrick's case, he didn't kill him," Mike suggested.

Mike hadn't talked to Brodrick yet, but he had heard through his teammate, Kenny, that he would be out soon. His mom had gotten him a lawyer and was paying his bail.

"I'm sure this will be cleared up soon," Mike added. He was standing firm. He wouldn't choose sides. Someone close to him was dead and someone else close to him was in jail. To him, there were no sides to choose from.

Mike thought back to the incident. He had helped Kenny push Brodrick away from Coach. Mike remembered thinking that Brodrick looked like he wanted to cry. Like there were tears in his eyes.

"What's up, man? What happened Brodrick?" Kenny asked.

"He think it's a joke. He's messing with my future!" Brodrick yelled while trying to get back to Coach Bobby.

Coach Black had just gotten Coach Bobby to stand up. Through his bloody and swelling face, Mike thought he could see a smirk on Coach Bobby's face.

"You're finished, boy!" Coach Bobby yelled across the gym.

Brodrick tried yet again to get away from Mike and Kenny's arms. Justin ran over to help. The three of them pushed Brodrick outside behind the gym. Brodrick paced back and forth while trying to catch his breath.

"What happened, man?" Kenny kept asking.

Mike and Justin looked at each other and shrugged. Only a few moments had passed before the ambulance pulled up next to Coach Bobby's Dodge Charger. Coach Black directed Coach Bobby outside toward the ambulance.

Coach Black glared at Brodrick, seemingly daring him to come their way. Brodrick was still pacing. The police pulled up while the ambulance drivers were cleaning Coach Bobby's face. As soon as they parked, he could be heard yelling, "You're going to jail, boy! Arrest him, Officer."

Brodrick didn't even protest. He gave his phone to Kenny and allowed the police to handcuff him. "Call my mama and let her know where I am."

The team stood there confused. Kenny, Mike and Justin could feel the invisible line that was drawn between them and those near Coach. The team watched the police leave and the ambulance driver talk to the coaches.

"Ay, what y'all need?" Rogue's brother walked down the alley, passing the boys. Mike knew he was referring to some type of narcotic as Rogue had mentioned him as the family's disappointment since he dropped out of college.

"We good, man," Mike walked into the gym. The other players followed.

A few moments later, Coach Bobby and Coach Black finally followed the players into the gym. Coach Black told them practice was over, and to go home and get some rest for the game tomorrow.

"That boy has gotten himself into a whole heap of trouble," Coach Black added. "Anybody seen Coach Bobby's keys?"

A few players helped Coach Black look around the bleachers where Coach fell. Everyone else just left. Including Mike. He had no clue that things could possibly end up the way they had.

"Alright guys, let's go," Mr. Whittington reentered the classroom.

"Where are we going?"

"Assembly time."

Everyone looked at Mr. Whittington, confused. "It's our turn to sit in with the counselor. Let's go."

The class followed Mr. Whittington out of the classroom and to the auditorium. Several hundred other students were already gathered inside. Each student shared the confusion of the next.

"We've called this assembly to address your concerns of recent events," the counselor, Mrs. Gresham, began. "We have indeed lost our beloved history teacher and varsity basketball coach, Coach Bobby. There was also an incident between Coach Bobby and one of our students, Brodrick Timmons, preceding Coach Bobby's death. We currently have no evidence that the two are related."

The students began to whisper to each other, causing Mrs. Gresham to speak louder.

"We understand your concerns and we want to offer our support. Please come by my office if you feel these recent events have become overwhelming for you. If needed, we will offer group therapy and we have access to outside professional therapists, if your needs are beyond our available care."

Mrs. Gresham nodded to the teachers positioned along the edge of the assembled students. They began passing out sheets of paper to each of the students.

She continued, "We have prepared a statement for you and your parents, along with a 24-hour counselor line, should you need assistance outside of school hours. I will also be available at the school until 8 p.m. for the remainder of this week and all of next week."

Mike glanced at the letter. It was basically the same thing Mrs. Gresham said, along with a list of websites and phone numbers at the bottom.

"Students, you may return to your classes, but I'll need all of the basketball players to remain in the auditorium." Mike looked up to see Coach Black standing at the podium.

4 DEANTE BLACK

How could he address a basketball team after what had just happened? The same team who corralled around the player who murdered his friend? Coach Black didn't want to address the team, but he knew that he needed to. He knew that it was the responsible thing to do, but if it wasn't for Mrs. Gresham, he wouldn't do it.

"Hey, guys." Coach Black's voice cracked as he spoke. He shifted, cleared his throat and then tried again. "Hey, guys. I know that we are the trending topic in the city right now. I understand that there's a hashtag referring to our situation."

Coach Black glanced over the ten or so students that sat in the front of the auditorium. His eyes rested on the student that he was looking for.

"I know with all of this attention, some of us may feel compelled to tell our story to the media. I want to ask that you refrain from doing that."

Once he noticed the other players eyeing Franklin. Coach Black's eyes continued to scan his audience. He continued, "There's a lot to sort out right now, but without any clear answers, please try not to speculate. Let's just allow our justice system to run its course."

Coach Black urged his students not to speculate, but he couldn't help doing so himself. He knew that it was Brodrick's vicious blows that killed his friend. Brodrick was 6'5", 235 pounds and had the largest wingspan in the district. Everyone knew that before basketball, Brodrick was an amateur boxer. He had even seen him knock out other students with one punch. Although all of those facts were convincing, what was most convincing to Coach Black was what he saw.

Brodrick had punched Coach Bobby in his face multiple times before he fell. Still not accepting that he had the upper hand, he had also kicked Coach Bobby until Coach Black was able to stand in between the two. Had Coach Black and the other players not intervened, Brodrick likely would have beat him to death right then and there.

The death was hard on Coach Black because all Coach Bobby had to do was listen to him. He had urged Coach Bobby to go to the hospital immediately after the incident. Brodrick was quick, but it was like Coach Bobby welcomed those punches. Coach Black didn't remember him block not one. He didn't even cower until he had fallen to the ground. Even the paramedics pled with Coach Bobby to allow a doctor to look at him, but repeatedly he refused. He had even planned to drive himself home.

"You're in no condition to drive, man," Coach Black tried to talk some sense into Coach Bobby after the ambulance left.

"My head hurts a little, but I'm fine. I've been in a fight before."

"What if your eye swells on the way there?"

Through the growing deformation, Coach Black detected a smirk. "I'm only three blocks away-"

Coach Black helped him finish the repetitive joke, "in the ugly green and yellow house on Clydesdale Street. Yea I know."

"You know I could walk there in ten minutes." Coach Bobby attempted to chuckle. "Besides, I have two eyes. I only need one to see."

"What has gotten into Brodrick lately?" Coach Black had asked. He wasn't sure what the fight was over, not that it mattered.

"You know how it is, man." Coach Bobby shuffled with his pockets. "You can take the kid out the hood, but you can't take the hood out the kid." He looked around. "Have you seen my keys?"

"Maybe they fell when you went down. The clipboard, your whistle, whatever papers you had with you were all on the floor. Let's go check."

Coach Bobby walked with Coach Black back into the gym and told the remaining players that practice was canceled. The clipboard, his papers and whistle were neatly stacked on the end of the bleachers, near the area where he fell. He helped him look around for a few moments, but his keys were nowhere in sight.

"I think this is a sign," Coach Black turned to Coach Bobby, "let's stop at the hospital, then I'll take you home."

"Home is a great idea," Coach Bobby responded. "How about you just take me home? You know I keep a spare house key by the door. And I'll go to the hospital later tonight if I'm not feeling too well after I get some rest."

Coach Black didn't agree, but he was tired of beating a dead horse.

"Really. What was up with Brodrick? That was totally uncalled for. What was he mad about this time?" Coach Black asked him on the way to his home.

"I told him he wasn't starting in tomorrow's game. He's all worried about the recruiters seeing him. You know it doesn't take much for that kid to get upset."

"Still. That was a lot, Bobby."

"Well, he'll have a good long time to think about it now. He can kiss his chance at the league goodbye."

"The league?" Coach Black questioned. "It's too early for that anyway."

Coach Black watched as Coach Bobby tilted the five-gallon Emerald

Green porch plant to retrieve his spare key. He unlocked the door, then returned the key to its conspicuous hiding place. He never thought that that key was a good idea, but Coach Bobby thought otherwise. He was more interested in having a safe haven for his students with accessibility to a clean home and stocked fridge. Or just a safe haven to get away from it all. That's the kind of guy Coach Bobby was. He'd give the shirt off his back if he thought it would help a student succeed.

This crossed Coach Black's mind as he tried to speak positively to his team. A team that included a kid that would hurt a man who did nothing but good for the students of their school. This made it hard for Coach Black to want to help. Clearly, these kids would literally bite the hand that fed them.

Coach Black tried to regain focus. "We are grateful that the district has allowed us to reschedule this week's game due to these unforeseen circumstances, but we will return to play next week. And we will play in Coach Bobby's honor."

Justin began to clap. The other players quickly joined him. Coach Black allowed them to clap for a few seconds before he continued. "I hope that we all find peace and tranquility during these trying times. But if you find that you cannot play next week, for any reason, please let me know. We will not hold this against you.

"Practice will not resume until Friday, but of course, you can take all the time that you need. Thank you."

Coach Black exited the stage while Mr. Whittington ushered the players back to their classrooms. He could tell by the look on several of their faces they wanted to talk to him, but he had mustered all the strength he could just to give that little speech.

Coach Bobby was not only his friend and his co-worker, but he was also his mentor. At fifteen years Coach Black's senior, Coach Bobby had not only given him professional tips, but he also gave him tips on life. Coach Black had spent countless times at his home, drinking a beer while Coach Bobby drank hot tea since he didn't drink alcohol. They would talk for hours about the best path for Coach Black's career, how to improve as a leader and coach, down to financial advice about saving for a home. It got to where Coach Black would run almost every important decision he'd make by Coach Bobby first.

Coach Black didn't know why he was so bothered by Coach Bobby's death. He wasn't sure if it was because they were friends, because he blamed the best player in the state, or because he was the one who found him dead.

Coach Black knew something was wrong when he didn't show up to work that Tuesday morning. He called him soon after he left his house to ask, once more, if he wanted to go to the hospital. He again said all he needed was rest.

"See you tomorrow, Coach." Those were the last words he had told him.

He didn't see Coach in his office that morning, so he figured that he was late. He didn't think much of it because he had his own class to get to. He knew that Coach Bobby taught a class after his, so he stopped by to check on him then.

The students were in their seats talking amongst each other, but Coach Bobby wasn't there.

"Where's Coach?" he asked Franklin, who sat by the door.

"I don't know," Franklin shrugged. "Maybe he's late."

Coach Black went straight to the office. He wasn't yet nervous, but he knew that was a way to get hard, cold facts. He texted Coach on his way to the office.

Where are you man?

Ms. Dewberry had just hung up the phone. She looked just as annoyed as she always had. "Hey, Ms. Dewberry. Do you know if Coach has been in yet?"

"Coach is popular today... huh?" she teased. "I just checked. He's not here."

Coach Black called Coach Bobby on his way to his car. Coach Bobby's Charger was still parked next to his, behind the gym. Coach Bobby had planned to walk to work that morning.

Coach Black got to Coach Bobby's house in record time. Coach Black snatched the single key from underneath the Evergreen pot. He called for Coach Bobby as soon as he cracked the door.

"Bobby? Bobby! Where are you, man?" He announced himself just in case he was inside the house.

His empty beer can and the tea cup were still on the living room table where they had left them the night before.

He glanced at the kitchen, which was directly past his living room, before making a left into the hallway. He looked past the open bathroom door before continuing to his bedroom at the end of the hall. "Coach! If you're back there, say something. I'm about to open your door."

With no surviving family, Coach had always declared himself an eternal bachelor. Although he had never known of Coach dating anyone, he wasn't looking for a surprise. Coach Black opened the door slowly, allowing time for Coach Bobby to protest. Once the door was completely open, Coach Black saw that Coach Bobby was sleeping peacefully, fully clothed, on top of the covers.

"Rise and shine, Coach!" Coach Black called. With each closer step, Coach Black grew more nervous.

Coach Bobby didn't stir, nor flinch, nor growl. He was completely unresponsive.

"Coach!" Coach Black's worry had grown to full blown terror. He shook Coach Bobby, but still there was nothing. He quickly dialed 911 while checking Coach Bobby's pulse with his opposite hand. Nothing.

"911," the operator calmly answered.

"Please send someone now! I think my friend is…" Coach Black didn't want to say it. He knew if he said it, that would make it real.

There was no way to take back the words once they came out of his mouth. He checked the other side of Coach's neck and then his wrist.

"Sir? How can I help you?"

"Dead," he finally responded. "I think my friend is dead."

5 CHEMERE JORDAN

"I heard that you were there, too." Lisa said to the new kid, Cam, with a lingering smile.

"Yea, but I didn't really see nothing."

"Brodrick beats Coach down and you're saying you didn't really see nothing?" She chewed her gum with her mouth wide open. She tried too hard to be sexy. Lisa swore she was the next big Instagram model.

She was starting to get on Chemere's nerves. "Shut up, Lisa," Chemere barked.

Lisa held her smile as she turned back around in her seat.

"Turn in your homework assignments now, thank you," Ms. Hall reminded the students from the front of the class.

Lisa took it upon herself to gather the few students' assignments who were near her and set them on Ms. Hall's desk.

"I know we've had a slow couple of days, but I still want to get you all prepared for your SATs."

A slow couple of days? Chemere thought to herself. She still couldn't believe that she hadn't talked with Brodrick. She didn't know what was going on. A few of the students conjured up some idea that he fought Coach on her behalf, but that was silly. Wasn't it?

She had always thought that Coach Bobby was a creep and had told Brodrick since the moment they started dating. He always brushed her off. Maybe he finally realized that his coach was a pervert.

She'd caught Coach Bobby staring at her a few times when he first came to the school. All the girls had a crush on him, so she thought it was cute at first. She'd even smiled back a few times, but that's because she thought it was innocent.

"You have some nice legs," he told her one day passing her in the hallway. They were alone. She was a volleyball player, long and lean. So, she was used to the compliment.

She simply smiled and said thank you. She felt honored that a man as fine as Coach Bobby, who could probably have any woman he wanted, was complimenting her.

The next time he spoke with her, it didn't feel so innocent. Chemere and a few friends were leaving late from a basketball game.

"Have a good night, ladies," Coach Bobby had said to them on his way to his car.

The girls thought the matte black Dodge Charger was an attractive car for an attractive man. They eyed him as he sat in his car with his windows halfway down and his music blaring. Chemere recognized her parents' favorite RnB oldie.

"Can we ride with you?" Lisa teased. The girls all giggled.

"We'll catch y'all later," one of the twins said as they both walked away.

"My mom's here. Do you need a ride?" Lisa turned to ask Chemere.

Chemere smiled. "No, I'm waiting on Brodrick."

"Mmhmm," Lisa joked. "Well y'all be safe." She left.

Chemere stood there alone, seemingly waiting to become a victim. Coach Bobby left his parking spot at the perfect time. No one entered or exited the gym when he pulled up in front of Chemere.

"Hey, pretty lady," he called.

She looked around casually before finally responding. "Hey."

He slowly looked her up and down. Chemere wasn't as curvy as some of her friends, so she didn't get much attention in her usual attire of a tank top, short shorts and flat sandals. But somehow, Coach Bobby's stare made her feel naked. "If you'd let me, I'd love to take you home."

"Um, Brodrick is taking me home," she said nervously.

"Well, if you ever need anything, my door is open for you anytime you want." He licked his lips slowly. "Anything you need. Just let me know."

"Thank you," she whispered before swiftly turning around to walk back into the gym. She instantly felt guilty because she was sure he watched her as she walked away. She just couldn't wait another moment. Never before had a grown man made her feel so uncomfortable.

Why did she smile at him when he first came to the school? Why did she accept his compliments? She started to think maybe he felt like she was leading him on.

"Your coach is weird," she said to Brodrick while he was driving her home.

"Why you say that?" He turned to look at her. He smiled. His light brown eyes flickered as he flashed his perfect teeth her way. His calm almost put her at peace.

"I always feel like he's watching me. He's kinda creepy." She tried to sound like it was no big deal.

"You are the one to watch," he casually glanced at her again. He softly brushed her hair away from her chin. He held his hand below her chin for a few seconds before finally turning back to the road.

It was that moment that she knew she was in love. She tried for weeks to avoid Brodrick's advances, but she couldn't stay away any longer. Too many girls wanted him, and she didn't want to miss her chance. She knew how much he loved basketball, therefore she didn't make a big deal out of his coach.

She called Lisa as soon as she got home. She needed another opinion.

"I felt dirty when he looked at me, Lisa. I'm telling you, it was weird."

"You felt dirty, huh?" Lisa asked sarcastically.

"For real, girl. I'm not playing."

"Okay. I'm sorry. What did he say again?"

Chemere explained every word, line for line. Even the excitement of having the star basketball player in the district drive her home wasn't enough to make her forget.

"You know he lets everyone come to his house, right? The basketball team, the students, everyone. That's probably all he meant."

Chemere didn't realize that. She had heard that a few students were going to Coach Bobby's house. They always called it some ugly-colored house on Clydesdale Street. She just always figured it had something to do with basketball. Chemere finally had enough information to make her think she overreacted.

Even if she overreacted, she didn't want to feel uncomfortable again. She did her best to avoid Coach Bobby whenever she could and if she couldn't avoid him, she'd avoid his eye contact. She focused her eyes on Brodrick during games and tried to avoid whatever area Coach Bobby was in. If she heard him in the hallway, she went the other way. She had gotten so used to avoiding him that she had almost forgotten about the incident.

"Is this your house?" Chemere asked when Brodrick pulled up to a small green and yellow house. Somehow, she expected more, but she wasn't one to judge.

"No. I told you I wanted us to spend some time alone. My mom's always in and out the house. This is Coach Bobby's house."

Chemere's anxiety returned without warning. It was the ugly green and yellow house the students often talked about. She looked at the street sign and sure enough, it read Clydesdale Street. "Oh no. I told you, he creeps me out."

Brodrick flashed his award-winning smile. "Seriously. What's the deal? Everybody loves Coach Bobby."

"I don't."

"Okay. I understand that. But he's not even here. I told you we'll be alone."

"I don't care, Brodrick." Chemere crossed her arms and looked out of the passenger window.

"Chemere," Brodrick's voice was softer. He put his hand on her chin and turned her face toward him. He waited until her eyes found his.

"Do you think I'll let anyone hurt you?"

Chemere sighed.

"I just want some alone time with you. Just a little. No noisy restaurants, no prying eyes, just the two of us for a few minutes."

Chemere thought about his words. It would be nice to cuddle next to him alone. To listen to his heartbeat with her head in his chest. To tell him her secrets while she listened to his.

"Remember, the teachers have a mandatory meeting after school. We'll be gone before he even gets back."

"So you have a key to his house?"

Brodrick jumped out of the car and walked around it to open the passenger door. He took Chemere by the hand as she slid out of her seat.

"He leaves a key under the plant, so we don't need a key. I told you, he's a cool guy. Maybe you just gotta get to know him."

Chemere shuddered at the thought.

Brodrick had some type of spell on her because it didn't take five minutes for her to feel comfortable again. Surprisingly, Brodrick was a complete gentleman. She expected him to try to do something with her. She even wanted him to, but he never did. She was surprised. He actually did want them to spend alone time together.

He turned on the television while she leaned against him on the couch. Two episodes of Martin had gone off before she found the courage to make the first move. She didn't want him to think she was easy, but she didn't want him to think he had wasted his time with her. It did take two weeks of him asking before she finally agreed to be his girlfriend. She loved the looks the other girls gave her when they found out that she was indeed Brodrick's girl.

She thought maybe she had heard something when she pressed up against Brodrick and slid her tongue in his mouth, but she didn't want to stop. When Brodrick quickly pulled her off of him, she knew something was wrong.

He stood up quickly to explain while Chemere sat nervously on the couch. She realized what a horrible choice she had made in coming to that house. Anything could happen to her now. She continuously tried to tell herself to think of an exit plan if needed. She hoped she didn't look as afraid as she felt.

Brodrick and Coach Bobby mumbled something to each other before Coach Bobby laughed and walked away. She looked up at Coach Bobby, which was something she hadn't done in months. In a split second, he made her feel just as uncomfortable as he had before. He winked at her, smiled and licked his lips as he walked out of sight. She jetted out the door the second he disappeared.

"I promise, Chemere. I have never seen Coach act that way before." Brodrick blurted as he started the car.

"I never want to be around him again. I told you. I told you that I didn't want to go in there."

"I know. I'm sorry. Let me get you home."

Chemere spent the entire ride thinking about what happened. Considering what could have happened. She hated the way her anxiety had often got the best of her, but she had to consider the consequences.

Brodrick could have set her up. She wouldn't know. He used to fight kids all the time and he seemed really loyal to his coach. He wasn't always this nice guy that she was falling in love with. What if Coach Bobby used his basketball team to lure kids to his house to do god knows what?

"Chemere. Please tell me what's going on in that pretty little head of yours."

Brodrick's full body was turned toward her. She looked around and realized that they were parked in front of her house.

She sighed, then placed her right hand on the door. Brodrick pulled her left hand into his. She turned to face him. He kissed her hand softly, then stared into her eyes.

"I really enjoyed spending time with you today," he said. "I'm sorry that Coach Bobby came in and made it all weird. That part shouldn't have happened."

Chemere loved the sentiment, but she didn't know what to say. So she didn't say anything.

"Our homes aren't the best places to meet up unless we're sitting outside. And I could get us a room, but I didn't want you thinking I just wanted you for sex. I wanted to find us a neutral place. Please accept my apology."

His eyes remained fixated on hers. The way he held onto her hand and looked into her eyes made her feel like she was in a love story. Every girl at Hamer wanted Brodrick. He messed with plenty of girls, but hadn't entertained a girlfriend since freshman year from what she had heard. And now he was staring into her eyes and asking her to accept his apology. She decided not to let her anxiety win this time.

"And I promise, if Coach Bobby or anyone else ever makes you feel that uncomfortable again, I will end it myself."

She smiled. The only man that had ever seemed to protect her like that was her father. "I accept your apology."

The night ended perfectly, and many more nights ended perfectly after that until the night Brodrick went to jail.

6 KENDRICK MOORE

Kenny really hoped Coach's death wasn't Brodrick's fault. Everyone had mixed feelings about the incident, including Kenny. He was there to witness the fight and although it was pretty bad, he just couldn't see how it could cause Coach's death. Sure, Brodrick hit him with an unrealistic, retro, Mortal Kombat combination, followed by some heavy kicks to his abdomen, but Brodrick wasn't trying to kill him.

He was definitely mad at him. He could tell that Coach Bobby must have taken his crass jokes too far this time. Everyone was at the funeral talking about how Coach Bobby was such a great man. They talked about how he turned a winning team into an undefeated team after only his first season. Kenny always thought they gave Coach Bobby way too much credit.

Hamer High might not have won all of their games in previous years, but they always went to State. Kenny knew, like most of the players felt, it had more to do with the team staying together three years in a row. They knew each other's strengths and weaknesses like they knew their own.

They knew when Frank started fouling the other players that he was tired. They knew when Justin came in quiet that he had had a fight with his mom. His anger made him play extra hard. Kenny would never admit it, but the players also knew that when he spent the evening with his girl, he'd lead the team in throwing up bricks. Coach wasn't some team magician.

"Coach," Coach Black was fighting back tears. "We will always remember the sacrifices you made for our team. The joy that you brought to our students and players."

Kenny was worried that he wore a disbelieving look while watching Coach Black, so he diverted his attention to the body in the casket. Although the funeral home did a great job preparing the body for the funeral, he could still see the bruising around Coach Bobby's eye and lip. He eyed his teammates on both sides of him. Some were fighting tears while others looked lifeless. He looked back up at Coach Black.

It was decided that Coach Black would say a few words on behalf of the team. Although well attended, no one expected the funeral would last long. Everyone in attendance had only met Coach Bobby when he started at Hamer High two years ago. Coach Bobby joined the team at the perfect time. Right when Coach Walker retired to a remote beach off the coast of East Africa.

Coach Bobby earned the respect of every player on the team and seemingly every student in the school. It wasn't because he was the great guy that Coach Black described. It was because his house was the hangout spot. Any given day of the week at any given time, students could pop up at the ugly, green and yellow house on the corner of Clydesdale Street. People may be sad about Coach Bobby's death, but they'd be even sadder about the end of the hangout spot.

After only forty minutes, the attendees gave their condolences to the basketball team on the front row. It was time for the starting players to carry the casket outside to the hearse.

Kenny dodged the looks of his classmates. He knew a lot of them thought it was hypocritical for him to be a pallbearer, carrying the man that they thought his best friend accidentally murdered. He felt weird about it himself, but how could he say no? As a matter of fact, when Coach Black approached the team, it wasn't even an option. They were just told that they would do it.

"The first two rows will be reserved for the basketball team and our starters will be the pallbearers." Coach Black laid out the funeral plans during practice earlier that week. "You all need to wear your dark suits that you wear on game days."

The players shared a few glances, but no one said anything. Not even Frank. Coach Black had taken over as the organizer for Coach Bobby's services as well as head coach. He took over everything as a father figure. A figure that no one asked for, nor felt they needed.

"Yo, why is Coach Black acting like that all of a sudden?" Frank asked after practice.

"You know he looked up to Coach Bobby," Justin responded.

"So what!" Rogue exclaimed. "We all looked up to Coach. That doesn't mean we want to take over handling his affairs."

"I don't think Coach had family," Kenny added.

"I can't believe he wants you to be pallbearer," Justin huffed while looking Kenny up and down.

Kenny buffed his chest and took a step toward Justin. "Why not?" he asked the rhetorical question.

"They waited a whole week," Mike interjected. His voice full of concern. "No one could find Coach's next of kin. Coach Black volunteered."

"All he asked us to do was show up in suits. It's the least we can do," Justin sneered at Kenny before leaving the gym.

It didn't bother Kenny that Justin was acting like a bitch. He knew that Justin ran behind Coach Bobby like his little pet. Coach had even tried to move him to start multiple times. He was a good player, but not good enough to start.

Although he tried not to show it, Justin took Coach's death the hardest. He often tried to take his anger out on Kenny because he was Brodrick's best friend. Kenny tried to brush Justin's attitude under the rug because knew how bad it would look if he too had a fight with another player on the team. Justin would probably follow in Coach Bobby's footsteps and let Kenny hit him, simply so he could play the victim.

Something wasn't right about the whole ordeal. The players said that the assault had something to do with Chemere, but Kenny wasn't convinced. Kenny didn't even think Brodrick and Chemere were that serious.

Kenny had been friends with Brodrick since middle school. The person Brodrick used to be and the person he was today were completely different. Or maybe not. Using his anger instead of his words was something that the old Brodrick would do. Coach Bobby must have said something to bring the old Brodrick back.

When Kenny first met Brodrick, everything pissed Brodrick off. The kid who was once angry at everything was the first person to welcome Coach Bobby with open arms. He eased the tension all the players had against a new coach.

Last season, when Coach first suggested that players could meet at his home, everyone was reluctant, but it was Brodrick who embraced it. Sometime after the new season started, something changed.

"That felt awkward as hell," Rogue exerted after Coach Bobby's casket was securely in the ground.

"I agree." Frank was serious, unlike his normal demeanor. "How do you bury someone with no family in sight."

"We're his family," Justin exalted.

"Yea, we get that Just, but where's his mom, dad, sister, brother, cousin, 4th cousin removed... anyone?" Kenny was growing tired of Justin's naivety.

"You don't remember," Justin said genuinely, "he didn't have any family. Coach Black tried. He contacted all he could, but he couldn't find anyone."

"Man…" Rogue added. "That kinda sucks. To just die alone."

"That's why it was important for us to be here," Justin declared. "We're his team and we let our teammate beat him to a bloody pulp. A lot of this is also our fault. The least we can do is see him off."

Justin caught up with Coach Black. Kenny assumed it was so he could catch a ride. And he was grateful he did. The players carpooled together and he didn't want to be around him another minute.

Justin increasingly made it a habit to fault Brodrick for Coach's death, but Kenny wasn't buying it. Although Brodrick didn't completely say it, Kenny had a feeling that there was more to the story.

He called Brodrick the night before the funeral. Surprisingly, he answered.

"What's been up, man? I've been calling you since you got out."

"I know. My lawyer doesn't want me talking to anyone else until this legal matter gets dealt with. He told me to save my story for court. I just wanted to let you know that I'm not trying to avoid you guys."

"Come on, you gotta tell us something."

"I'm not even supposed to be answering my phone right now. My mom would kill me if she knew."

"Everyone is saying you're an accident murderer."

"I already know about that stupid hashtag. I don't want to hear about what everyone is saying, bro. I gotta let you go. Soon as I get the clearance, I'll hit you up. Just make sure you tell Chemere."

Brodrick hung up the phone. Kenny was pissed. Here he was, trying to help Brodrick's name and he didn't even care.

Kenny didn't loosen his anger until Justin walked away. Mike, Rogue and Frank were still standing next to him. Rogue lit his cigarette.

"Y'all know Coach wasn't some saint," Kenny said.

"Hell naw, he wasn't no saint," Rogue managed before releasing his smoke. "I think he was banging Lisa."

"I don't know if he was banging Lisa, but I'm pretty sure he was all up in Ms. Johnson." Frank laughed.

Kenny looked from Frank to Rogue. "Are y'all serious? I heard he was banging that neighbor chick."

All three boys started laughing. Rogue's laughs ended in a cough.

"Man, why do you smoke those things?" Frank asked.

"It helps me cut the drugs."

"Yo brother got you too, huh?" Mike asked.

"So, you're trading one bad habit for another?" Kenny questioned.

"I got a misdemeanor. No matter how hard I work, I can't make it to college like ya boy," Rogue said. "Hell, I doubt he even make it now, with the drama he's facing."

"Aw man…that's right," Frank added. "There's so much happening, that I hadn't even factored in how this affects his college offers."

"And to think, college was just to bide him so he could go pro," Kenny mentioned. It hadn't even dawned on Kenny that Brodrick's promising future would be over from his sudden act of violence. "That would make more sense if his college or professional future is what made Brodrick flip."

"You might be right," Rogue took his last puff, "but I'm sure he'd have a much better chance had he kept his hands to himself."

"Excuse me, gentlemen." Kenny turned around to the sound of the small voice. There was a portly, disheveled man approaching them. "I'm working on a story about Coach Bobby and I understand that you guys are all players on his basketball team."

"We don't talk to reporters," Rogue responded without even looking at the man. He threw his cigarette butt on the ground before squishing it into the dirt with his shoe. "Any of y'all need a ride?" he asked while walking away.

Mike followed Rogue. Kenny glanced at the man's narrow eyes before following Mike. He heard Frank's footsteps right behind him.

Do either of you think his girlfriend did it?" The man called behind them. "It appears she was the last one to see him alive."

Kenny stopped walking. Frank stopped next to him. They both looked at the man in disbelief. Pleased with their attention, the man walked toward them.

"Don't listen to him, man," Kenny heard Mike call behind them. "They'll say anything to get a story."

Kenny waved the man off. He caught up with the Rogue and Mike in the parking lot.

"Ay, my mixtape, Sounds of a Real Dude, is on Spotify, Google and Apple. You know, anywhere you get your music," Frank ran to catch up with the guys. "Mention that in your story. Tell everybody."

7 BRODRICK TIMMONS

Brodrick hated that Coach Bobby was dead. Not because people thought that he had killed him, which he knew he didn't, but because no one should have to die unexpectedly.

Coach was a hater, a bit inappropriate, and somewhat disrespectful, but he didn't deserve to die. At least that's what Brodrick told that blogger dude. He agreed to see him the day he got out of jail.

The reporter, Natalia Randle, had originally planned to meet him, but then passed him on to the blogger dude. Although Brodrick would have preferred to tell his story to the local newspaper, he was happy to at least tell his side of the story. That way, people could stop with the stupid hashtag. Even if his mom and his lawyer disagreed.

Brodrick was already seated when the guy showed up.

"Thank you for meeting me." The blogger dragged two chairs while trying to squeeze between the café tables, catching the attention of half the diner.

Brodrick towered the man when he stood to shake his hand. "No problem," he said as they both took their seats.

"What did you say your name was again? I'm sorry, but I'm bad with names."

"My name is Chancellor, but just remember me as *Underground News*."

"Is that where the story will run?"

"Yes. Check us out online." Chancellor searched three pockets and his briefcase before finding what he was looking for. "We're also on all social media platforms."

Brodrick examined the card. "Yea, you're the one who started that hashtag, accident murderer, right?"

"No. Actually, we didn't start the hashtag. Someone just posted that under our story. Like Natalia told you, we only want to get your side."

"Well, you agreed to not mention my name, right? This is off-the-record?" Brodrick remembered hearing that term when watching crime TV.

"Yes, of course. I never betray a source." Chancellor propped his laptop on the table. "I'll just type my notes as you talk."

"Can I get you guys anything?" The waitress's lip curled as she eyed Brodrick.

Chancellor adjusted his glasses while focusing on his screen. "Coffee, please," he shrieked.

Brodrick smiled at the waitress. "Bottled water."

"Coming right up." She twirled away.

"I don't have long. I'm only supposed to be picking up lunch."

Chancellor finally peered above his laptop to face Brodrick. "Do you know if Robert has a drug problem?"

"Who?" Brodrick didn't understand how Natalia Randle was friends with this guy. She was so well kept. Not a hair out of place. This Chance guy couldn't even get his facts straight.

"Your coach?"

"Coach Bobby…" Brodrick said slowly. Making sure to emphasize Coach's name. "Did not do any drugs. He's an athlete."

"Hmm…" Chancellor began to type.

"Here ya go," the waitress set a mug of coffee next to Chancellor's laptop. She extended Brodrick's water toward him. Once he acknowledged her, she smiled. He caressed her fingers as he slid the water from her hand. "Let me know if you need anything else," she winked.

"Was the fight over your girlfriend?"

"What!" Brodrick snarled.

Chancellor glanced at the puzzled look on Brodrick's face, then he turned to look at the waitress until she walked away. He casually grabbed a stack of sugars, ripped them open, and poured them into the mug. "Why did you fight your coach? Was he messing with your girlfriend?"

"Naw. This has nothing to do with my girlfriend. Coach was trying to mess with my future."

Chancellor annoyingly stirred the coffee in his mug. "So, why'd you beat him?"

"I don't like your line of questioning. I thought you were here so that I could tell you my side of the story."

"Published in *The Elite Telegram*, you had a fight with your coach on a Monday. He refused medical attention. He died on Tuesday and his funeral is tomorrow. Those are the facts. The public knows all of that, but they don't know why you did it. So, why did you do it?"

Brodrick could feel his anger rising. He tried to remember to breathe. He tried to remember to think before he spoke. He did neither. "I didn't kill my coach!" he blurted. The flimsy table rocked as he stood.

Several heads turned his way. His eyes found the waitress. Her admiration turned to surprise. Chancellor sipped his coffee before hacking away at his keyboard.

"What can you tell me that *The Elite Telegram* and, therefore, the entire city does not already know? You're out on bail. Could be awaiting a new charge. Now is the time." Chancellor stopped typing and let his eyes follow Brodrick as he returned to his seat.

"I can't talk about my charges," Brodrick whispered across the table.

"I didn't ask you to." Chancellor sipped from his mug.

Brodrick studied Chancellor. He didn't so much as raise an eyebrow. His demeanor was calm. It was the opposite of Brodrick's. Maybe it was because they were in a public place, or maybe he had asked these kind of questions to people all of the time. He almost seemed disinterested in Brodrick.

"This is very informal and as you said, off-the-record. So what can you tell me about your coach?"

Brodrick took a deep breath. He tried to remember all of the coping mechanisms he had learned from counseling. After three years of weekly appointments, he'd often joke that he had only learned how to breathe. Something that was so natural, yet he'd often forget to do when he was upset.

"Coach and I were cool. I really looked up to him when he first came last year."

Brodrick almost relived his pivotal moments with Coach Bobby. He told Chancellor about all the compliments Coach would give him after the games. How he couldn't believe that Brodrick was such a great basketball player and that he was honored to be coaching the next LeBron James.

"He was almost like a father figure, but don't tell my dad I said that." Brodrick chuckled, trying to break the tension. Tension that, apparently, only he felt.

Chancellor took turns typing and sipping, but never interrupted Brodrick's story. It reminded Brodrick of his counseling sessions.

Brodrick told how Coach would allow all of the players and their friends to hang out at his house. It started as an after the game thing, so that the players wouldn't hang out in questionable areas, but it soon became an all-the-time thing.

"Yo, Coach," Brodrick remembered his teammate Justin saying, "I wish we could hang out over here all the time."

"Why can't you?" Coach replied.

The team was reluctant to hang out with their new coach, until Brodrick convinced them otherwise. At least thirty kids from the school were there that day. They used Coach's credit card to order pizza. Someone had brought a few beers. Someone else had connected their phone to a Bluetooth speaker. It was an instant party.

Coach stood and faced the students to make sure all of them could hear. "Mi casa es su casa! For real, any of you can come by any day at any time. Whether I'm here or not. Consider this your safe haven."

The students all laughed and smiled. Brodrick thought that was the coolest thing he had ever heard an adult say. Soon after, everyone looked forward to hanging out at the ugly green and yellow house on the corner of Clydesdale Street.

After that, Brodrick could often hear students say, "Meet me on Clydesdale Street."

To Brodrick, Coach could do no wrong. If any student, player or otherwise needed anything, Coach wouldn't hesitate to get it for them. He let the students know that there was a spare key at his door that they could use at their disposal. Many students took him up on that offer.

It took over a year before Brodrick started questioning Coach Bobby's generosity. He'd often thought back on the day he started looking at Coach different.

He had met up with his new girlfriend, Chemere, at Coach's house. They went immediately after school because they knew the teachers had a mandatory staff meeting. They would only meet up to have alone time, or at least that's what Brodrick had told Chemere.

Students had access to the guest bedroom, but Chemere wasn't having it. She kept saying that she didn't feel comfortable. Brodrick hadn't been dating her long, but she never felt comfortable being around Coach Bobby.

The two were making out on Coach's couch when he walked in. Both Chemere and Brodrick jumped when Coach opened the front door. They pulled away from each other.

Brodrick stood, ready to explain himself. "Oh, I'm sorry Coach-"

Coach interrupted him. "Don't stop on account of me," he smiled. "You two can do whatever you want, if you let me watch."

Brodrick was confused. Then he was upset. Before he could say anything, Coach let out a huge laugh.

"I'm just joking. Never mind me. I'll be in my room." Coach disappeared into the hallway.

"I told you he was a creep," Chemere rushed past Brodrick and walked out the door. He caught up with her on the sidewalk.

"Take me home now!" she demanded. He took her home and they never talked about that day again.

Brodrick took a deep breath and a huge gulp of his water.

"Do you know if he ever slept with any of his students?" Chancellor asked.

Brodrick sighed. "Man, I hope not." He shook his head. He realized the picture he was painting of his coach. He knew Coach Bobby would sometimes say inappropriate things about female students and teachers, but he didn't think he would actually do anything inappropriate.

"That's the thing," Brodrick continued, "He would just say stuff, but I don't think he meant any of it."

Brodrick thought about another time the whole team was at Coach's house. It was the beginning of the season. They gathered to watch videos of the rival team before the next game. The meeting started on basketball, but when Coach left to the kitchen to get more salsa, the conversation had somehow transitioned to the guys asking Brodrick about Chemere.

"I guess she my girl. She always hanging around me." Brodrick knew that Chemere was his girl because she had finally agreed after weeks of him asking. The guys didn't need to know the details, though.

"Aw! Justin, I guess that means you'll never get that chance to lose your virginity to her," Frank joked.

"I ain't checking for that girl."

Everyone knew that was a lie. He had been the butt of a bad joke since she declined the flowers he had delivered to her for Valentine's Day.

"And I ain't no virgin."

"Oh yea?" Frank teased. "Who?"

Everyone looked at Justin, waiting for an answer.

"You wouldn't know her."

"Yea, I bet," Frank started his goofy laugh and a few players joined in with him.

"I been a G. I started banging my babysitter when I was in middle school."

"Yea, right!" Frank smirked. "You were driving Miss Daisy?"

"Bro," Brodrick interrupted. "That's rape."

"That shit ain't rape," Justin declared. "She had just graduated high school. I got game like that."

"Yea, you tripping bro," Mike added.

Coach Bobby had reentered the room. "Don't hate on him, Brodrick, because he can pull his babysitter." Coach had given Justin a high five.

Brodrick was conflicted. As an adult, Coach should have known better. It took an entire year of therapy before Brodrick realized that his own babysitter was the root of his anger and another year to realize that her violation caused him to distrust all women. Although no one knew it, getting a girlfriend that he liked and trusted was the project that he had started with Chemere. It was hard for him to shake his bad boy image. But he didn't want to hide behind his anger anymore.

"Come on, y'all," Brodrick wasn't letting it go that easy. "If what you're saying is true, Justin, that girl took advantage of you. How old were you, like twelve?"

"For real, Brodrick. Chill out. This isn't law and order." Coach Bobby grew serious. "Let's get back to basketball."

"As an adult, you should be the main one telling him that that's wrong."

The boys looked from Coach Bobby to Brodrick. That was the first of many times the team would try not to pick a side.

"Now you want to question my adulthood. What would you know

about being an adult?"

"I know an adult should be protecting students, not telling them that it's okay to be used."

"Oh yea?" Coach moved closer to Brodrick. "Well I'm such an adult, I'm going to tell this little boy to get out of my adult house."

Brodrick stared at Coach for a moment. Their faces were less than a foot apart. Brodrick stared long enough to know that Coach was serious. He glanced at the confusion of his teammates before grabbing his backpack and slamming the door on his way out.

Brodrick never talked about that incident again, but the relationship between him and Coach would never be the same.

"Many of our comments say that you fought him because of your girlfriend…um…" Chancellor's eyebrow raised. Brodrick watched as he pulled a small group of disheveled papers from his bag. He thumbed through the papers carefully before looking back at Brodrick. "Chemere?"

Brodrick was confused, "What? She has nothing to do with any of this."

"So, what made you hit him?" Chancellor interrupted his thoughts.

"I had a plan. Coach was trying to mess up the plan. I don't know why, but when I found out, I just snapped."

"What kind of plan?"

"A good school, possibly the pros, you know… the whole nine. Life-changing plans, man."

Brodrick stopped talking when he felt his phone buzz in his pocket. He answered it quickly when he saw the name.

"You better not be talking to that reporter!" his mom exclaimed.

8 ANDY KURRIN

The Hamer High team wasn't the same without their star basketball player and their winning-streak coach. If this was the sendoff the team was having for their deceased coach, it was not a good one. Andy had been to several of Coach Bobby's basketball games, but he was sure this game would be his last. Andy remembered the first call he got from Bobby at the beginning of the season.

"I was going to call the folks at Duke, but I figured you needed a win. I would love to be modest, but I'm telling you. Right now, I'm coaching the next LeBron James," Coach Bobby convinced.

"I've seen the stats, but nothing is jumping out at me. Maybe later in the season," Andy had heard the spill before.

"No problem, Andy. I'm sure the players that Joe doesn't want will be excited to talk to you then. You have a nice day, you hear?"

"Now, hold on Coach Bobby." Andy didn't know many high school coaches who knew that his rival's assistant coach did the bulk of their recruiting. And if they did know, he doubted they knew that he was affectionately called Joe by his friends. "I'll actually be in the southwest this weekend. I can stretch my visit to stop by for your Tuesday night game."

Andy thought to himself, *what could it hurt*? Though it wasn't originally a priority, he knew that the 5A high school had a few potential prospects. Most notably, power forward, Brodrick Timmons.

The trip proved to be successful because Timmons was actually better than Andy had originally thought. Andy slid into the game behind a small family, trying to blend in. He hated when players or coaches noticed who he was and tried to impress him.

The game was already intense with the rivals barely gaining more than three points against each other. Andy assumed that the man wearing the cobalt blue jumper, running up and down Hamer's sideline was Coach Bobby.

"Come on, B!" the man yelled.

The six-foot-five power forward grabbed the flailing basketball from the air. Andy knew it was Timmons from the number three on his shirt. Timmons boxed out his six-foot-three opponent. In one fail swoop, the basketball found the net and the crowd went wild.

Rushing to the other end of the court, the team in black found their offensive positions. The ball handler slowed his stride to identify the best move for the play. He looked right, but he threw left and Timmons stepped right around the offensive player to steal the ball. Timmons quickly threw the ball to player number five as he sprinted down the court. Player 23 double-timed to the top of the circle, where the basketball flew to meet him. Another three points were earned in a matter of seconds. The gym erupted. The black team called a time-out.

If there was one thing Andy loved, it was good, clean basketball. No matter who played it. He watched Hamer's team listen intently to the long, seated man on their sideline. Andy would soon learn that this was, indeed, Coach Bobby.

"Good game Coach," Andy said as he walked up to the man in the cobalt blue jumpsuit at the end of the game.

"Andy Kurrin," someone called from behind him. He turned around after he finished shaking Coach Black's hand.

"I'm Coach Bobby." Coach Bobby extended his hand to Andy.

"Good game to you as well."

"I'm happy you could come out to see my boys."

Coach Bobby had him meet the entire team, but he focused more on Brodrick Timmons. Brodrick was a stern player who didn't seem easily impressed.

"Nice to meet you, Mr. Kurrin," Timmons said while releasing his firm grip. "Kentucky's a great school, but I don't know much about their engineering program."

Coach Bobby interrupted Timmons with a laugh. "He's just joking with you." Coach Bobby patted Timmons on the shoulder. "You boys go get cleaned up."

Timmons looked a little confused, but he complied. He waved to Andy as he followed his teammates to the locker room.

"You hungry?" Coach Bobby asked him.

It wasn't the first time Andy had come across a student who seemed more interested in their studies than basketball. He was, after all, recruiting for a college. Although he admired those types of players, they weren't his most favorite to recruit. It was harder to get academically focused players to understand the magnitude of the required commitment. They would look at their practice and game schedule and somehow still think they could pile on 18 hours of classes.

Coach Bobby insisted that Timmons' first love was basketball. He said he had at least three players who were college ready, but Timmons was definitely his best. Timmons could go straight to the NBA, he said. Andy distinctly remembered him saying that at the beginning of their season, but somewhere along mid-season, that had changed.

"I don't know if Brodrick would be a good fit for Kentucky," Coach

Bobby told him just a month after he visited.

Andy figured he was entertaining other college recruiters. He was always prepared for this part of the game. "What do you want?" Andy asked, trying not to sound annoyed.

"No, Seriously. I don't think he has the discipline to even go to college."

Andy couldn't believe it. "You trying to get him in the G league, aren't you?" Andy scoffed. He talked with Timmons and his mom several times and they both were adamant about him getting a good education. He had finally convinced them that Timmons would want to take it easy his freshman year because his basketball scholarship had player requirements. Timmons really got excited about seeing his face on national TV.

"Of course not, man. A good player has to have good sportsmanship too and right now, I think he's negatively affecting the team."

Andy was confused. Timmons seemed to be one of the most humble players he had ever met. Timmons knew that he was a good player, but he didn't gloat. He could tell that he took a lot of thought into his future and his actions. Coach Bobby was painting a completely different picture of his star athlete.

"I don't understand. I thought we were really on to something. I got the entire staff here excited, presenting him as a prospect."

"I'm just warning you," Coach Bobby sighed. "What you decide is your choice."

Andy hung up the phone confused. He knew of high school players with bad attitudes, poor grades and who had come from bad families. Neither of those described Timmons. Timmons was an only child to divorced parents. Both parents were pretty well off. To his parents, basketball was simply a hobby. Andy always did a temperature check with potential prospects when getting to know them.

"How do you react when an opposing player says something nasty to you?" he asked Timmons once when visiting their two-story home in a gated community.

"I used to get really angry. Even fight them." Timmons looked at his hands when he spoke.

"MMhmm," his mom could be heard murmuring from the couch.

"But now," Timmons looked up, "I don't let it get to me. I've learned to do a better job of not reacting to everything thrown at me. I haven't had a fight in over a year," he said with a smile.

Andy had never really seen anyone say something like that with such joy. "Well, that's good," he said. "We play good, clean, basketball. We don't want to recruit any bad boys."

Andy was convinced that Coach Bobby had some other issue. He had even asked Timmons the very next time he talked to him.

"How's everything with you and Coach Bobby?"

"It's good."

"What about the team?"

"It's cool. Why do you ask?"

He didn't want to throw Bobby under the bus. Andy quickly remembered a fact that he could use as his excuse. "Well, you're not putting up as much per game. I've been looking at your most recent stats."

"Coach been trying to give other kids exposure. He said I don't really have anything else to prove and he's right. Some of our other players need more playing time."

Andy was even more confused. Timmons sounded like he and his coach were on good terms. He tried just once more.

"How is the spirit of the team? Is everyone excited about the bench getting more playing time? I know that can cause a little animosity against players."

"I mean, no one likes it. Especially when I get put back in at the end of the game and have to work harder for the win. But it's a team sport, so what are we to do?"

Andy didn't think Timmons sounded upset at all and he made sure to let Coach Bobby know that the next time he called.

"Did you get that email I sent you?" Coach Bobby had asked.

"I hadn't had a chance to look at it. I've been doing a lot of traveling. What was it? Some clips?"

"Yeah. I want you to check out one of my other players, Justin. He's really improved. May be something that you're looking for."

"We already have our eyes on Timmons." Andy remembered Justin. He wasn't a very good player, but Coach Bobby insisted that he had just been overshadowed.

"What's made you change your mind? I talked to Timmons just last week and he seemed as upbeat as he had always had. Didn't seem like he was having issues with the team."

"Andy, I see him every day. You saw him what? Twice? I know I promised you greatness and I don't want it to backfire on me. Coach to coach, he's really just not a good fit. I didn't want to leave you empty-handed, which is why I'm showing you Justin."

"I appreciate the sentiment." Andy said it, but he didn't mean it. The behavior was weird and he was finalizing a package to present to Timmons just that week. "But we're at the home stretch. Just between me and you, we're ready to aggressively ask Timmons to join us."

Coach Bobby sighed. "Look, I didn't want to say anything, but Brodrick is facing several assault charges. I know how important it is for you to sign players who are a good fit."

"We've already looked into his previous record. Everything checked out." Andy wasn't a fool. He knew better than to recruit any kid based on their word. His previous cases had been expunged. Information that neither Timmons nor his mom had to divulge, yet they did. "Did something new happen?"

"Well…" Coach Bobby lingered. "There's been rumors amongst the students that he may have sexually assaulted someone."

"What? Rumors?" Andy didn't know if he should be angry or grateful for the information. But rumors weren't enough to silence this deal. "Has he been charged? Arrested?"

"No, not yet. I don't know if the student will actually press charges."

"Well, if this student presses charges, let me know." Andy hung up the phone. He tried to get the thought out of his head, but he was still thinking about it two days later.

"Hey Andy, what's up?" Timmons answered. Andy waited until the end of the school day to call.

"Um, Timmons? There's something that's been on my mind that I want to talk to you about."

"Shoot."

"Are you getting in trouble over there?"

"In trouble?" Brodrick laughed. "I just made the A honor roll."

"I heard a rumor that you may have sexually assaulted a student." Andy didn't know how else to say it. He didn't plan to say where he'd heard the rumor, but he had to ask.

"Where'd you hear something as absurd as that?" Timmons chuckled.

"I just want to be sure that everything with you is still the same."

"Wait? Are you serious?" Timmons tone had deepened. "Someone actually told you that I had sexually assaulted someone?"

"I just want to be sure. That's all." Andy could tell that Timmons was insulted. He instantly felt upset with himself for calling. The last thing he needed was to create any type of tension between himself and this prospect.

"I think you need to seriously check your sources. I have worked hard to improve my reputation. Maybe had you said physical assault, I would have thought someone simply got their facts crossed. But sexual assault? Really? I do nothing but play basketball, study and hang with my friends. And I have a girlfriend. Who would I sexually assault? Definitely not her?"

"I really am sorry. This information came across my desk and I thought it was best to check with you first."

"Well, I at least appreciate that you came to me first. But you can call my girlfriend, ask my friends, coach, even my teachers. I would never do anything like that."

Andy apologized profusely and he made sure Timmons wasn't upset when he ended the call. Timmons said that perhaps it was karma for the players that he used to fight. Then he asked Andy again to do more research on his background if he thought he was a liar.

Andy had no clue what would cause Coach Bobby to tell him something like that. Nothing had come of the sexual assault rumor, but he soon found out Timmons had assaulted Coach Bobby.

Everything about the ordeal was eerie, including the weird guy that called him from *Underground News*. The man called him one afternoon after he heard about the coach's death.

"Hi, um…can I speak with Andy Kurrin?

"This is he. How may I help you?"

"It appears Brodrick Timmons is no longer being charged. Is he still a prospect for your school?"

"Who is this?"

"We've been told that he's no longer a suspect in the case about Coach Robert Maker. Are you still considering him as a scholarship recipient?"

"It doesn't matter if he is a suspect. We don't need that kind of press at our school. Who is this?"

"So is it safe to say that the next Lebron James should find a new path to the NBA? Is your offer completely off the table?"

"It doesn't matter. We never officially presented our offer anyway. Are you going to tell me who you are or do I have to hang up on you?"

"Just a concerned basketball fan, sir."

"Well goodbye, concerned basketball fan." Andy hung up. That was exactly the type of drama he couldn't afford to bring to his organization.

9 LETICIA HALL

Those stupid blogs were getting out of hand. Leticia wished someone could stop them. She thought the students calling Brodrick an accident murderer was bad, but it seemed the stories were getting worse. It had been weeks and the topic wasn't old news yet. It was hard to console her friend if the city would never get over it in the first place. Jameson didn't even come to work that day.

Leticia had been friends with JJ since she joined the teaching staff three years before. She wouldn't necessarily consider them best friends, but she definitely thought JJ was her closest friend at the school.

It bothered Leticia that JJ had a mild obsession with Coach Bobby. Leticia was the only one JJ confided in about their secret relationship, and she had only done that by accident. Once Leticia found out, it seemed JJ spent every moment they had together talking about him.

Ironically, anytime she was around Coach Bobby, he never mentioned her.

Leticia and JJ would often meet in the lounge before school and had a habit of eating lunch together a few days a week. Occasionally, they'd hang out by the pool of JJ's apartment complex. Those fun times were becoming annoying as JJ couldn't help but gush over her newfound love. JJ gushed about Coach Bobby so much that Leticia didn't even think she noticed.

"Have you been to that new sushi place? Bobby loves to have lunch with me there," JJ said one afternoon during lunch.

"Girl, I'm sorry I missed you this morning. I got in a little late. Bobby kept me up all night," JJ whispered one afternoon in the lounge.

Leticia overlooked most of JJ's comments because she knew she was just young and in love. She could remember feeling that way about a guy when she was JJ's age. It wasn't until she overheard Coach Bobby talking to Deante that she tried to give JJ relationship advice.

"My sister and her friends were checking you out at the game, Coach." Deante and Coach Bobby were talking after the staff meeting.

"Why don't you slide all of them my number?" Coach Bobby laughed.

"Naw, seriously Coach. Don't you ever think about settling down? My sister's friend, Janaye, is a real good catch. I could introduce you."

84

"To be honest, Deante, I'm not the settling down type. I date here and there, but I'm married to the game of basketball."

"Good evening, gentleman." Leticia made her presence known.

Both turned around to acknowledge her. Coach Bobby winked, "Hey, Leticia."

She ignored him. His pretty face got her once, but he wouldn't get her again.

She wanted to stop JJ in the middle of her many rants about Coach Bobby, but didn't want to sound like a hater. So instead, she tried giving sisterly advice. It took a lot of convincing, but she once talked JJ out of surprising Coach Bobby with a weekend trip to Vegas for his 45th birthday.

"I don't know, JJ," Leticia urged. "That sounds like a great boyfriend gift, but don't you think you two should go public first?"

"I know it seems sudden, but I know he cares about me like I care about him."

It took everything in Leticia not to roll her eyes. She knew that simply disagreeing with a woman about her man could potentially ruin a friendship. "I really do think it's a good idea. Maybe as a Christmas gift. Just give it a little more time."

"You may be right."

JJ's naivety really reared its head the day she found out that she wasn't the only person that Coach Bobby was dating. A truth that

Leticia had wanted to allude to since her friend decided to cozy up to the coach.

"It makes sense now," an exasperated JJ explained. "I've been wanting to go public with our relationship since we decided to be exclusive last month. He kept putting it off."

"But didn't he say when you two first started dating that he didn't want a relationship?" Leticia tried to get her emotional friend to think rationally.

"That was then. You know that we've been together every week. Almost every day since then." JJ was fighting back tears. "To think. I was going to pay for us to go to Vegas and everything. That's a lot on my salary."

Principal Rich walked into the lounge. JJ turned her back to him.

"Good morning, ladies," he said. He glanced from Leticia to JJ's back.

"Good morning, Mr. Rich." Leticia looked him in the eye to hold his attention.
"Is she okay?" he whispered to Leticia.

"Allergies," she shrugged.

JJ continued to clean her face, while Leticia made small talk with their principal. It only took moments for him to finish pouring his coffee, then leave.

"Look, JJ," Leticia scurried to her friend. "You have got to get yourself together. You two have only been dating what? Six months?"

"How can he love me, yet he's texting someone else?" Tears streamed down her face.

"Do you need to go home for the day?" Leticia didn't see how JJ was going to teach a class in the state she was in. They only had ten more minutes before the next class began.

JJ told Leticia that she had stopped by Coach Bobby's office after they talked that morning when she saw a text come through his phone.

Can't wait to see you, was what the text said. Coach Bobby explained it away, but Leticia could tell that JJ's intuition told her otherwise.

"I'll be fine." JJ sniffled. "But this isn't over. I'm going to talk to him this evening and show him what happens when he plays with my heart." JJ's sorrow had turned into anger. "He thinks he can hurt my feelings?" Her face was now a scowl. "No one hurts me and gets away with it," She seethed through gritted teeth, then stormed out of the lounge.

Leticia knew that JJ was full of empty promises laced with harsh tones. She was younger and identified more with a generation that conversed in emojis and thought phrases such as *going dumb* and to *get stupid* were fun terms instead of demeaning labels. If they hadn't found out about Coach Bobby's untimely death the following morning, Leticia was sure that she wouldn't have even remembered JJ's words.

Leticia looked for her friend as soon as she heard about Coach Bobby.

She briskly walked down the halls of Hamer High and noticed a still figure in Coach Bobby's empty classroom. She walked into Coach Bobby's classroom to find a shocked JJ, frozen in motion.

"Oh my god JJ, I just found out."

JJ stood still with tears slowly crawling down her face. The teaching staff had spread the news within minutes, followed by a confirmation from the principal.

"I'm so sorry that this has happened. Are you okay?"

A chirp alerted Leticia that she had a new message. She soon heard JJ's phone chirp immediately after. She read the message on her phone.

Mandatory staff meeting in the library.

"We just got this message about a mandatory staff meeting. I'm sure it's about Coach Bobby. We have to go see what's going on."

Principal Rush confirmed again that Coach Bobby had passed. There was no update on what happened, but it appeared that he had died in his sleep.

"We don't have time to prepare statements to send home with students, so please keep this information confidential. We are working closely with the police department to issue the most accurate details when we make our statement in the morning."

The teachers all shared a look of shock and sadness.

"Please return to your classrooms as soon as you can. We don't want to alert the students prematurely."

Leticia made sure JJ had someone to console her before getting to her class. She was happy Mr. Rich gave them time to adjust to the startling news before having to address the students' concern.

"Ms. Hall, how much time do we have?"

A student broke Leticia from her thoughts. She looked at the clock and realized that it was fifteen minutes over the time she had given students to complete their quiz.

She smiled, "I figured y'all needed some extra time. Trade papers with your neighbor."

The students made an entire event out of selecting the appropriate peer to pass their quizzes to.

"Miss," Leticia heard a student call from the back.

She hated when students called her Miss. As if they hadn't had her as a teacher for months. She was one of the most senior teachers in the school. Everyone, including the parents, knew her proper name.

She stood up to make sure she addressed the right student. "Yes, Lisa."

"Were you listening to us? Do you think Ms. Johnson did it?"

Leticia was confused. "Did what?"

"Killed Coach Bobby," another student answered for her. She looked to see that it was Rogue who spoke.

"What?" Leticia was baffled.

"It's on the blog site, Miss," Lisa added. "It says Ms. Johnson was the last person who saw him alive."

"It also says they were dating," Rogue completed.

She could hear a few snickers and confirmations from the other students.

"I hope y'all paid attention to finance the way you are to rumors."

"Ms. Hall, you have to know the scoop, though," Rogue said.

"You guys can gossip on your own time." Leticia was determined to remain professional, but everything inside of her wanted to know what the students were talking about and who was blaming JJ and for what exactly?

Leticia wondered if this is why JJ didn't show up to work. She wondered who else could have known about their relationship. She had been checking with her every other day to make sure she was fine. She even escorted her to the funeral service. Was she being accused of something?

She hated to question her friend, but things weren't looking so good. She found that blog story as soon as school was over. The details in the story were alarming. The tone of the story was stunning, but there was one part that Leticia read over and over again.

Jameson Johnson, fellow teacher and secret lover of Maker, was the last person to see him alive the night of his death. Friends close to Maker say Johnson had been stalking Maker for some time and that he could not be reached via phone immediately after Johnson left.

Leticia knew that JJ must have been livid. Leticia dialed JJ several times, only to hear the phone going straight to voicemail. She rushed to her car soon as the last bell rang. JJ's home was out of the way, but considering the current circumstances, Leticia didn't mind.

"Did you know about this?" Deante charged toward Leticia in the parking lot. There was a single sheet of paper in his hand.

Surprised, Leticia turned to face him after opening her car door. "Huh?"

"This article from *Underground News*."

"That's not an article. It's a blog post," she corrected him.

"Was Ms. Johnson dating Coach Bobby?"

"I don't know," Leticia lied. She was cool with Deante, but she wasn't cool with spreading anyone else's business.

"You're her girl. You should know."

Leticia decided that she didn't like his tone. She was going to end the conversation, but he spoke first.

"Didn't you date him last year, too? What, are y'all just passing men around?"

Leticia forgot she had told him that. That was back when Coach Bobby first came to the school. Before he and Coach Black had gotten to know each other and had become friends. He was one of the few people who knew. JJ didn't even know. It wasn't necessarily a secret, but there was a level of decorum teachers tried to maintain and him questioning her in the parking lot was beneath that level. It was borderline disrespect.

"I know that you're upset, but don't speak to me in that manner." Leticia scowled. "Even if any of that is true, what does this have to do with you?"

"Bobby died two weeks ago. I was the one who had the unfortunate experience of finding out, but even through that horror, I shared that information with all of you. The least someone could have done was let me know that I wasn't the last person who saw him alive. That there was someone else there who could have helped."

Leticia was starting to empathize with Coach Black.

He raised an eyebrow and turned up his nose. "Unless they have something to hide."

Empathy disappeared. "Okay, I'm done with this conversation." Leticia slammed her door and drove off.

She unsuccessfully dialed JJ several more times before reaching her apartment and beating on her door.

"It's me, JJ. Open up!" she yelled at the door. She knew she was home because her blue Mazda was in its designated parking spot. After five minutes and several ugly snarls from JJ's neighbors, JJ finally opened the door.

"What's going on?" Leticia asked while helping herself into the apartment.

"Everyone is talking about you withholding information about being the last person to see Coach Bobby alive. Why didn't you say something?"

JJ still had on her headscarf. Leticia figured that she must've stayed in bed all day. "Everyone is making a big deal out of nothing," JJ sighed. She sat in her oversized sofa.

Leticia sat on the loveseat, opposite the couch. "You didn't even tell me. Now, Coach Black thinks you're hiding something."

"Who cares what Coach Black thinks?" JJ's lifeless voice was raspy.

"Are you okay? Are you going to tell me what happened?"

"Nothing happened, Leticia. I went over that night to check on him and he said he was fine. He just wanted to get some rest. So, I left."

"How come you've never said that before?"

"Because nothing happened."

"You went all the way to his house and just left? I remember you said that you were going to hurt him that day."

"Really?" JJ looked at Leticia. She looked through Leticia. She turned away to look toward the arm of the loveseat. Tears began to stream from JJ's eyes. "I wanted you to think I was going to break up with him. You always judge me when it comes to him. And now you think I had something to do with him dying."

10 GLORIA TUCKER

Gloria knew that the teacher lady killed Bobby. She tried to hint that information to the police, but it seemed to go nowhere. Bobby had always told her that the lady was crazy. Gloria told her husband and the other neighbors, but it seemed no one would believe it. It almost made Gloria feel like she was the crazy one.

She saw the lady she now knew as Jameson the night of Coach Bobby's death. She heard Jameson's car door slam and crept to the window to peer out. She ensured that her bedroom light was off, so no one would notice.

The Jameson lady clicked her lady of the night heels briskly to Bobby's door and waited. A few seconds later, she retrieved his key from under the beautiful Evergreen that Gloria had bought for him when he first moved in. She always told him that letting so many people have access to his home was a bad idea. Jameson had to have been in the house for a full twenty minutes before sneakily creeping out. Gloria wanted to call Bobby right away, but her husband interrupted her.

"What are you doing in here with the lights off?" He turned on the bedroom light and walked in.

Gloria moved away from the window. "I was just about to come downstairs. I heard a noise, so I went to the window to see what it was."

"What kind of noise?" Her husband studied her face.

"Oh, a car door or something," she said without thinking. She brushed past him to go downstairs.

"A car door? We hear those every day," she heard him say behind her.

She knew that her husband was growing suspicious of her and he had good reason to. She tried her best not to add to his suspicion. She had had an affair with her neighbor, but it only happened once. Well, actually twice. It could have been more like three times, but she definitely tried not to make a habit of it. She and Coach Bobby were actually more of friends.

Gloria was a lonely housewife and an empty nester after having only one adult child. She easily grew tired in finding interest in simple things. She planned parties for her neighbors, attended a weekly book club, volunteered as a secretary at her church, and whatever else she could find to keep herself busy.

It wasn't often that people moved in and out of the neighborhood, so she was excited to see a moving truck in front of the house next door about two years before. She became aroused when she learned that her new neighbor was a basketball giant, chiseled to perfection with a smile that instantly melted her heart.

She had asked her husband to escort her next door, so that she could meet the neighbor and deliver her perfectly baked apple pie. Her husband declined to join her, just as she hoped that he would. She really wanted to see this man up close without her husband's watchful eye.

He answered the door before she finished knocking. "Hello," he said with a divine smile.

Gloria was shocked at his demanding presence. He stared at her intently. Somehow, his dark brown eyes glistened. She glanced over his perfect hairline, the thick arch in his brow, then over his strong jawline. His manicured mustache connected to his small beard, framing his full exotic lips. The man was perfect.

Suddenly, Gloria felt embarrassed. She was afraid that she wasn't enough to be standing in his presence. Although her dress was fitted, her pout was perfect and she smelled like a floral bouquet, she felt that the thought she put into that moment wasn't enough to impress him. He was sweaty in what looked like an old basketball T-shirt that said Hoop Dreams.

"How may I help you?" He spoke with patience and smiled with his eyes. He seemed pleased with her standing there; that although she didn't look like the beauty queen that she knew he deserved, he wanted her on his doorstep in that moment.

"I. Um…" Gloria looked for the appropriate words. "I brought you pie." She immediately wanted to retract her statement. It wasn't sexy or purposeful. It sounded dumb.

"Oh." He looked at the pie in her hand. She held it right below her cleavage. He leaned in and took in a deep whiff. "That smells delicious."

She pushed the pie toward him and forced an awkward smile.

"I don't eat sweets, but it won't go to waste. I'm going to take this to my students tomorrow. I'm sure they'll love it."

He covered his hands around hers. She blushed, then gently slid her hands away. She glanced at her red wedge heels before finding the confidence to look back into his awaiting eyes.

"Your students?" she questioned.

"I'm sorry. My name is Bobby." He held the pie in one hand so that he could shake her hand with the other. The pie looked so small in his hand. "I'm the basketball coach at Fannie Lou Hamer High. I also teach history there."

"Oh." She smiled bashfully. "My name's Gloria. So, you're teaching at my alma mater."

"Did you just graduate last year?" He smiled.

"Oh, of course not." She giggled. Although it wasn't necessary, she appreciated the compliment. Her beauty regimen ensured that she didn't look a day over 35, but high school was an obvious stretch. Perhaps it meant that he thought she was attractive. She playfully pulled a few strands of her bob behind her ear.

"Do you bake for all of your neighbors?" His eyes remained locked into hers.

"We don't get new neighbors often. I just wanted to make sure you felt welcomed."

"Would you like to come in?" He opened the door wider, but kept his eyes focused on hers.

"Oh no." She brushed the hair that was no longer there away from her face; this time, using her left hand to make sure he saw her ring.

"Well, you're welcome here anytime."

She blushed again. "Thank you.

He stepped backward into his foyer while still smiling at her.

"Now that I know you don't eat sweets, I'll have to bring something else for you."

"I appreciate the gesture, but you don't have to. You simply stopping by with this pie made me feel welcomed enough."

"It's my pleasure."

He nodded to her before softly closing the door.

Gloria took a deep breath before walking back home.

"How's the new neighbor?" Her husband called from the couch as she walked inside the house.

"He's the basketball coach at Hamer High," she replied, deliberately sounding disinterested.

"That's nice."

Her husband didn't even look up at her and she was grateful that he didn't. Her light brown cheeks were probably beet red. She couldn't shake the dreamy look in her eyes or the smile spread across her face.

She spent her days replaying those moments in her head. She fantasized about the perfect thing to give him that wasn't a dessert. Maybe forgoing food altogether was better. She had to give him something else. Something special but not too special because, of course, she was married. She didn't want him to think that anything could happen between them. Nothing would happen between them. She was sure of it. But what harm was it to simply fantasize?

She picked up an Evergreen plant while out shopping. It made her smile when she thought that he may think of her whenever he saw it. It was something that would last much longer than any pie would. The next time she visited Bobby, she made sure it was when her husband wasn't home.

It took two days for that perfect moment to arrive. It was a Saturday morning, during her husband's routine fishing outing. She knew he would spend hours on the lake, so that gave her enough time to prepare. She looked out the window to make sure the matte black Charger was parked in the driveway, then she got herself together.

This time, she wore tight fitted jeans and a low cut blouse. Her only pair of stiletto pumps would have to do. She marched right over to Bobby's house. She pressed the doorbell once and waited a few seconds, but there was no response. She pressed it once more, but there was no response again. She felt silly for making a fuss for a man that was probably too busy to even notice her.

She bent down to set the Evergreen on the porch. That's when the door opened. Bobby stood there, bare-chested and rubbing his eyes. He yawned.

"Good morning." He sung with outstretched arms.

Gloria popped up. "Oh, I'm sorry. I didn't mean to wake you."

Bobby smiled. "No, it's okay. I was just about to put on some tea." He left the door open and walked away. "Come on in," he called back to her.

She looked around nervously. No one was outside. No one would see that she walked into a half-naked man's house. She quickly picked up the Evergreen plant and clicked her heels right in.

She looked at the unmatched furniture and stacked boxes against the wall. She spotted him in the kitchen.

"Have a seat." He nodded toward the bar stools on the other side of the bar.

The home had an open floor plan. Past the entrance, the living room was to the left, the dining room to the right and the kitchen toward the back. All could be seen standing in one spot. Gloria would soon learn that the bedrooms were just past the living room, down a small hallway.

Bobby filled the tea kettle with water and placed it on the lit stove.

"Come on. I won't bite." He smiled.

Gloria slowly walked to the bar and set the Evergreen on top of it. He set two teacups in front of her.

"Give me one second. I need to put on a shirt."

He drifted past the living room, down a small hallway. Gloria was grateful, although she knew that his bulging chest would linger in her thoughts later. The sight of her being alone with him half-clothed made her uncomfortable. She never planned to cheat on her husband.

That day was the beginning of their friendship. They talked for hours about Hamer High, basketball and neighbors. Gloria considered her and Bobby to be really good friends. She'd often hang out with him on Saturday mornings when her husband was away and they'd talk or text on some evenings. It was mostly innocent. She had only slept with him a few times over the course of the two years she knew him. She wasn't looking to mess up her marriage. Bobby was just a guilty pleasure that she learned to trust. A friend who filled a void that none of her other friends could.

Bobby felt that Gloria was a good friend of his, too. That had to be why he would confide in her about details in his personal life.

He told her about his joys and faults with coaching at Hamer. How he made friends with the teaching staff and his passion for making a safe haven for students.

Gloria grew to love seeing the students over all during the week. They seemed overjoyed to be there and were very respectful when they saw her outside. She had even ordered pizza for them a time or two. What she wasn't fond of was seeing the young teacher who would stop by.

"So… I've seen that small, blue Mazda out front several times this week," Gloria said to him one Saturday morning. "Are things getting serious?" Her eyebrow raised over the teacup she sipped from.

"You're so nosy." Bobby chuckled. "She has been over here a lot though, hasn't she?"

"I thought she may have moved in." Gloria said it jokingly, but hated to admit to herself that she was jealous. The young lady he affectionately called JJ had to have been a Pilates instructor. Every time she stepped out of that ugly blue bug, she looked flawless. Much too fancy to simply be a Sociology teacher, and she looked much too young to be one, too. The first time Gloria saw her, she thought she was one of the students.

"I think she's starting to use my kindness as a weakness. I don't know a nice way to tell her to leave me alone."

"Maybe there is no nice way. Direct may be best."

"Sometimes, she pops up unannounced, too. She's even calling me almost every day. You would think we were dating." Coach Bobby looked exasperated.

Gloria didn't know why, but she was happy to hear him say that. She had to keep reminding herself that she was married to the love of her life, although the love of her life seemed to be married more to his job and that damn TV. "You are such a charming guy." She smiled at him. "I'm sure it comes with the charm."

He returned the smile. His piercing eyes always made her look away first.

"You have to make sure she understands if you don't want to be with her. You know a woman scorned can do some pretty ugly things," Gloria warned him.

That had to have been only a month or so before his death. Gloria wished she said more. She never thought such a small girl could do harm to such a big guy, but now she thought differently. She imagined that he tried to end it and she just wouldn't take no for an answer. Maybe if Gloria was more adamant or if Bobby wasn't such a charming person, he'd still be alive.

11 JUSTIN PLOWMAN

Coach was a saint, and it was like everyone was forgetting that. Just because Coach's death seemed to be something more complicated than Brodrick's murder didn't mean he wasn't the great person that people had come to know. And Justin couldn't understand why some random blogger was going to lengths to destroy Coach Bobby's name.

"I told y'all my boy didn't kill Coach," Kenny blurted in the cafeteria one day.

"It says why he beat him, not that he didn't kill him.," Justin added.

"Did you read the same story everyone else read?" Kenny looked at Justin like he had shit on his face. It seemed to Justin that Kenny had an issue with everything he had to say.

"Brodrick beating on him didn't help," Justin reiterated.

"He tried to sabotage his career. Are you serious?" Kenny snapped.

"What do you think happened to him?" Mike questioned.

"Clearly, it was Ms. Johnson. She was obsessed with him and was the last one to see him alive," Frank added.

"Naw, I can't believe that," said Kenny.

"She probably found out about him and that neighbor chick," said Mike.

"Or Lisa," added Rogue.

"Coach didn't deserve to die like that," Justin added.

The guys shared glances before looking back at Justin.

"What?" Justin asked.

"Nothing, man," Kenny said with a sigh of irritation. The guys all waved Justin off.

"Whatever, man."

Justin's teammates always rubbed him the wrong way. Kenny always disagreed with him, and talking to Kenny was just like talking to Brodrick; those two were always together. Justin was sure he'd seen Rogue's brother around his mom feeding her addiction. Either way, the team didn't have enough empathy. They often said they weren't choosing sides, but clearly they stood up for Brodrick and spoke ill of

Coach. Justin didn't understand it.

Coach was really a good dude. Justin knew the guys were just hating on him because he was becoming Coach's favorite player. It's not like Justin was a kiss ass. He and Coach had become close on accident. The irony was that it was Brodrick who convinced the team to give Coach a chance in the first place.

Justin was in no hurry to rush home after their first game against the Moors in the beginning of the season.

"What's up, man? Why you still here?" Coach asked. Justin didn't realize that Coach hadn't left yet.

"I just want to get a little practice in."

"Naw. Really. Why are you still here?" Coach wasn't buying his lie.

"I'm just in no rush to go home, that's all."

"Why not?"

"There's nothing for me there."

"You know my house is always open."

"Yea, okay." Justin shot another basket.

"Seriously. You can ride with me or if you need time to think about it, remember I'm only three blocks away. The key is always under the plant."

Coach left the gym. Justin thought about it for a second. He would never tell anyone that his mama was a heroin addict, a habit she had only picked up since the government had come down hard on doctors who prescribed heavy opioids. An addiction she would have never gotten if she didn't hurt herself at work, a job she wouldn't have to work 12 hours a day if his father wasn't the piece of shit he was and actually helped her out. Justin didn't know who to blame, but he did need a safe haven. Basketball gave him that but once games were over, what was he supposed to do? No one really cared about a six-foot, sixteen-year-old African American kid.

He decided to take Coach Bobby up on his offer. He crashed on his couch that night and several nights a week. He had all the sports channels, and there was always food in the fridge. There was even the occasional beer available for him to consume when Coach wasn't there. He thought Coach would be mad when he spotted the finished beer can on the dining room table one night when he fell asleep on the couch.

"Did you drink that?" Coach asked a groggy Justin. He had just awakened from what he thought was a ten-minute nap. He rubbed his eyes clear to see what Coach referred to. No one had been in Coach's home all evening, including Coach. It was obvious that the beer can was his. Before Justin calculated his response, Coach spoke. "Don't down too many of those. You don't want that affecting your game."

All Justin could do was nod. Although his mom was an addict, she would have had a fit if she saw him even attempting to consume any type of drug, including alcohol. His mom's condition wasn't his only issue. Struggling to seem normal in the face of trouble was becoming harder for Justin.

Justin had been wearing the same basketball shoes all year. The rubber on the heels was beginning to wear and the paint had started to fade. His shoes started affecting his game. He missed a pass that Mike had thrown to him one day in practice.

"What the hell, man? How many times have we run this play? You know where you're supposed to be."

Justin knew the play like the back of his hand. Mike ran down the court while Justin would post underneath the goal. He'd collect the ball and shoot to Brodrick the second it touched his palm. He wasn't the one who normally ran the play. Coach finally gave him a shot after he continuously pled to be a starting player. Justin wasn't sure if he had earned his shot or if it was simply because Brodrick wasn't his favorite player anymore, but he didn't care. Coach was convincing the team by having him practice their normal plays, this play being the simplest, and he bombed it. He got there, but the lack of rubber on his shoes wouldn't let him stop.

"I know. My bad." Justin glanced at his shoes. Mike followed his gaze, then filled his face with a look of disappointment. He shook his head before looking over at Kenny.

Kenny looked from Justin's shoes to his face. "Let's just run the play again," Kenny said.

That day, Justin knew he needed to give up on basketball. Basketball made him feel good, but he needed to work to have the right equipment for the game. There was no way that he could do both. He felt sick thinking of the inevitable decision that he had to make.

He wasn't religious, but he normally went to church with his mom on Wednesday nights. He'd do anything to make sure she stayed busy. He decided to forego church that night to tell coach the upsetting news.

When he got to the ugly green and yellow house on Clydesdale Street, he saw Coach's car in the driveway, but the door was locked. He grabbed the key from underneath the Evergreen plant. When he walked in, the place looked empty. Justin figured that Coach was sleeping, so he made himself a sandwich and sat down to watch ESPN.

Justin was caught up on the game highlights when he finally heard a door open from the direction of the hallway. He didn't think anything of it until he heard a giggle. Justin sat up on the couch.

"You need me to take you home, Sugar Bear?" he heard Coach Bobby ask.

"Naw, it's cool. I'll just walk."

Justin was shocked to see Lisa emerge from the hallway. It didn't take a second for him to notice her waist-length hair and perfect stage make-up. Coach was right behind her.

"What's up, Justin? I didn't realize you were here." Coach announced calmly.

Lisa gave Justin a half smile and turned to give Coach Bobby a quick wave before leaving out the front door.

"I needed to talk to you," Justin mumbled. Justin had let himself into Coach's house many times, but this was the first time he felt like he shouldn't have. Maybe he should have called first. Or knocked. Maybe he shouldn't have used the key. Why did Coach always make sure to leave that key there?

"Cool, what you want to talk about?"

Justin forgot. He watched as Coach Bobby sat on the chair opposite the couch. He glanced at the TV before turning back to Justin. Coach was calm. Justin didn't know why he was the one that felt so anxious.

"You okay?" Coach looked into Justin's eyes. His facial expression almost worried.

Maybe it was all a figment of my imagination, Justin thought. Clearly he was making a deal out of nothing. All the students knew that Coach Bobby had an open door policy. Maybe he was helping Lisa with her homework or something. That would make sense. Wouldn't it?

"Were you helping Lisa with her homework or something?" Justin asked barely above a whisper.

Coach was nonchalant. He turned his head and thumbed toward the hallway before looking back at Justin. "Yea. She said her computer was broken. I told her she could just take one of my laptops, but she just did her work in the guest room. She told me she was finished, so I was just walking her out."

Justin's eyes were lost in thought as he made Coach's story make sense.

"I almost forgot," Coach said as he stood. "Don't you wear a size 12?"

Coach left down the hallway while Justin remained lost on the couch. He returned with a bag and gave it to Justin. "I was going to donate these to Goodwill, but wanted to see if you wanted them first."

Justin was happy to look into the bag. It stopped him from having to make eye contact with Coach Bobby.

There were two boxes of tennis shoes. Justin opened each box to learn that they were brand new basketball shoes in his size. "You said you were giving these to Goodwill?"

"I don't need them anymore."

"Did you ever wear them? They look brand new."

"I haven't worn them in a long time, but they're not new. I mean…if you don't want them, can you drop them off at Goodwill for me?"

"No, it's cool. I appreciate this." Justin wondered if someone told him that he needed shoes. Coincidentally, the shoes matched the team uniform.

Justin knew it wasn't just him that Coach helped. He gave students rides whenever they needed it. He'd even let a few players drive his car before. He was working on getting every senior a full-ride scholarship to top tier colleges. Coach did so much for the team. He did even more than their last coach and he was only there for a short while. Justin hated that it seemed only he and Coach Black took his death so seriously. He couldn't believe his own team would turn their backs on their coach. Coach would have never turned his back on them.

12 JAMESON JOHNSON

JJ couldn't believe that Bobby was dead. JJ thought she and Bobby were the perfect couple. Her petite frame, perfect skin, and hourglass shape hadn't changed much since her high school cheerleading days half a decade before. Although Bobby was twice her age, his long, toned, sculpted frame reminded her of her high school boyfriend.

Bobby was madly in love with her, too. He told her this often. She only had one issue with Bobby. He didn't want to tell anyone about their relationship.

"Why don't you want people to know that we're dating?" she asked one evening after hanging out at her place.

"I just don't think it's anyone's business," he responded.

The two had just finished dinner and retired to her apartment because it was nearby. It was always nearby because it seemed that her area was the only place they'd hang.

"I'm starting to feel like you just don't want people to know about me. Like you're trying to hide me."

"Baby, just give me some time. Let's keep enjoying each other and see where this goes first. Things get all complicated when we let people know that we're together."

"I don't need to see where this goes. I know how I feel now. I thought you felt the same. And besides, it feels like we're hiding something from Principal Rich. At least he should know."

Bobby gave her a kiss on her forehead, then smiled. "You worry too much, baby. Stop worrying. You know how much I love you. We'll let him know when it's time."

JJ really wanted to protest but he kissed her again, this time on her lips.

"Besides, you promised me dessert." He squeezed her butt from underneath her dress. He picked her up and laid her down on the loveseat. It became such a habit that the loveseat often reminded her of him.

JJ smiled at the memory, then frowned. He always did that. Every time she had something important to talk about, he'd find a way to change the subject. He'd always smile and act like it was no big deal, only to never discuss it again.

It took her months to realize that he was always evasive. She didn't want to make a big deal out of it because she had been verbally assaulted in past relationships before and Bobby never so much as raised his voice at her. He always smiled and told her that he loved her. He was perfect, except that he didn't want people to know about them.

They went on dates every week, usually after the games on Tuesdays and Thursday evenings. She was faithful to her yoga commitment on Mondays, Wednesdays, and Fridays. Bobby claimed her side of town had the best restaurants, so they were always near her house. She had only been to his house a handful of times and most often, not for very long. One day, she started to get suspicious.

"How come we always spend time at my house and hardly any time at yours?" she asked him.

"You know my house is for the kids. Think if one of them popped in and saw us together?"

"But they shouldn't really have access to your house the way they do anyway." JJ thought about the things some of the other teachers said when they found out that Bobby allowed students at his home. She wasn't sure if the news had reached Principal Rich yet, but she didn't think he would allow it.

"Some of these kids need a safe haven. They should always have a place to go where they feel comfortable."

"What about school? Home?" she asked.

"Those would be great places, but some kids have poor home situations and are bullied at school. You know that."

"I just don't know why this needs to be your job. I think in the long run, it will cause more harm than good."

"If I can make just one kid feel more comfortable in their skin, I think it's worth the risk."

JJ remembered feeling proud of him for being such a helpful person. She often wished there was more she could do to help the youth. She resented his assistance after learning that Brodrick had hurt him so badly. At first, she was shocked thinking that her favorite student was the reason for Bobby's death, but now everyone thought it was her. All she did was check on him. He was alive and well when she left.

She had already canceled her Monday yoga plans and fretted sitting in her quiet home worrying about her dying relationship. She decided the best way to stay busy was to stay at school longer. When she finally finished grading papers and planning lesson plans, she decided to leave for home. On her way out, she overheard students in the hallway talking about the fight.

She tried to reach Bobby immediately, but the call went straight to voicemail. She decided to quickly drive over to his house before leaving. She did wear heels and a fitted skirt that day, intending to impress him.

JJ was fuming when she pulled up to his house and didn't see his car.

She thought maybe he went to Sugar Bear's house. Wherever that was. After all, she *couldn't wait to see him. He did just have a fight,* she thought, *maybe he drove himself to the hospital.*

She then noticed his nosy neighbor peeking through an upstairs curtain. Bobby had once told JJ that the lady was an incessant flirt. She decided right then to strut right up to his door, sashaying her hips in her six-inch stiletto heels to give the neighbor something to see. She realized that was probably the worst idea. That neighbor had to have been the one who told the police that she was there because she hadn't told anyone else. But that shouldn't even matter because she didn't kill him.

She waited a moment after knocking. She always knocked first. There was no answer, so she did what she normally did. She retrieved his key from under that ugly plant his nosy neighbor gave him and unlocked the door. Everything looked normal when she walked in.

"Bobby!" she called a few times.

There was a single beer can sitting on the living room table next to an empty teacup. She knew the teacup had to have been Bobby's, *but who had the beer,* she wondered. She thought she heard a sound come from the kitchen. From where she stood in the living room, she noticed his keys on the bar, but the kitchen was empty.

"Bobby! Are you here?" she called again as she headed toward the long hallway.

She opened his bedroom door slowly to see him fully dressed, lying in bed. "Bobby," she called once more.

He stirred a little. She met him at his bedside.

"Hey, what's up baby." He managed a smile from his swollen lips.

"Oh, Bobby. Did Brodrick do this to you?" She knelt beside him on the bed.

He sat up. "I've been putting ice on it." He motioned to the ice pack that sat on the nightstand next to his bed. "I really just need to get a little rest. I'll be okay."

A huge purple and black bubble covered his right eye. There was a small cut above his left eye, sealed with dry blood.

"I can't believe he did this to you?" She purported.

"Some angel, huh?" He scoffed.

She ignored his reference to her praising Brodrick for being a model student athlete. "How do you feel?"

"I just have a little headache. I'm trying to sleep it off."

"Let me get you some medicine." She scurried to the bathroom in the midst of his protest. She grabbed a small bottle of ibuprofen and set the bottle on the nightstand next to his phone and the ice pack. "Let me get you some water." She turned to leave and he grabbed her arm. She turned back around to face him. "What is it?"

"Baby, I'm fine. Really."

She sat on the bed next to him.

"I'm happy you came to see me," he said.

Somehow, he still managed an intense stare deep into her eyes. She felt her admiration and love for him growing. The love and admiration she tried to bury since her argument with him. She turned away to avoid being hypnotized.

"I just wanted to make sure you were okay, but I meant what I said earlier." She said with her back to him.

"I know, baby. I didn't mean to upset you. We're going to sort this all out."

She turned back to face him. "Let me at least get you some water, in case you decide to take those pills."

She rushed off to the kitchen. She was about to look in the pantry for bottled water, but stopped short in a chuckle. He often teased her about her water choice. He called her bourgeois because she liked room temperature water. He preferred his cold. She grabbed a bottle of water from the fridge and returned to stand at his bedside. She was not going to stay with him.

He covered her hand with both of his while looking into her eyes. He placed the water next to the pill bottle with one hand while holding onto her with the other. "I've had time to think about what you said to me, and I promise that I'm going to make it right. I can't live without you. Okay, baby?"

He looked so sincere. She was tired of falling for his trap, but she could feel his charm through his mangled face. She wanted to love him through it all. She felt like a fool.

"Okay," she responded.

"Now, let me get some rest. I'll see you at work tomorrow."

"You really think you're going to make it to work?" She smirked.

"I know no one has ever touched your pretty little face before, but this was truly just a fight. I'll be there. Everyone will have a chance to see what your favorite student did to me."

She knew what Brodrick did was wrong, but she didn't think it served any good to make him look even worse. According to the students, he was already in jail. She didn't voice her thoughts. Bobby did need his rest. She would talk to him about it another time.

"Okay. I'll see you tomorrow," she said.

She locked the door as she left. He was fine when she left and although she was insanely upset with him before that day, he found a way to make her fall back in love in those brief moments they spent together at his house. Possibly, the last moments he spent with anyone.

If he hadn't been so reluctant about keeping their relationship a secret, people would have more empathy for her. They wouldn't accuse her. They wouldn't have questioned if she killed the man that she was madly in love with. The only regret she had was that she didn't tell more people about their relationship.

She often swore to Bobby that she hadn't told anyone about their relationship but she had, in fact, told just one person. One person had to know how happy she was and why she often smiled, even on a bad day of work. Her person was Leticia Hall.

"Something is fishy about Coach Bobby," Leticia confided in her one day.

"What do you mean?" she asked innocently.

"He never truly admits it, but I've overheard the students talk about going to Coach Bobby's house. And throwing parties at Coach Bobby's house. And meeting at Coach Bobby's house. That's not normal."

"Maybe he wants to use his house as a safe haven?" JJ blurted, repeating Bobby's words.

Leticia gave her a knowing look.

JJ had often looked to Leticia as a mentor. She had often told her things about teaching that she didn't learn in school. She was usually non-judgmental and had the gift of comforting her when she got down about the students.

"Are you dating him?" Leticia whispered as she approached JJ carefully.

"It's obvious, huh?" JJ shrugged, then looked at her hands.

"Oh, wow. How long has this been going on?" Leticia's tone was steady. She was inquisitive, but non-invasive.

At that time, JJ's relationship was only a few months old. She had taken up Bobby's offer for drinks one day and they had been involved every week since then. He told her that he tried to steer away from dating co-workers, but he had fallen in love with her. He needed to make sure it was real before committing. She told Leticia all of this, but Leticia wasn't buying it.

"Be careful," Leticia would tell her that day and each day that she gushed like a school girl, replaying her time with Bobby.

"I think I want to give him a key to my place," JJ had mentioned to Leticia the morning before the incident with Bobby and Brodrick.

"Really?" Leticia didn't hide her shock. "Do you think he would do the same?"

"We spend most of our time at my house anyway. Besides, he keeps a copy of his key by the door. I've used it several times and he's never complained."

"But didn't you say that he still doesn't want to tell anyone about your relationship? It's been what? Six months now?"

It had actually been closer to a year, but JJ didn't want to admit it. "Yea, but he loves me and I love him. I can see it every time he looks into my eyes."

"Do you even think he wants a key to your place?"

JJ wouldn't admit it, but it was actually Bobby's idea. He had mentioned several times that he'd like to pop-up at her place like she did his, although she had only done that two or three times. He vaguely mentioned a surprise waiting for her after her evening yoga class. Waiting for her to be done at 9:00 p.m. kept him from visiting her on those days.

"I think he'll be okay with it."

"I just think you should think about it a little more first. Maybe at least let people know you two are together."

JJ had already made a copy of her door key, but she knew Leticia's suggestion wasn't a bad idea. She gave her next class reading instructions and told them that she'd return shortly. She knew that it was Bobby's planning period, so it was the perfect time to go into his office.

His door was open, but he was away from his desk. She noticed that he left his phone by his computer. She figured he likely ran to the restroom because no one left their phone alone that long. She decided to wait a few minutes.

She thought of how she would approach him. She thought maybe she should show him the key and dangle it in front of him while asking that they go public. She'd tell him it was his if he'd tell Mr. Rich. She reached into her pocket to retrieve the key. That's when a short buzz from his phone caught her attention.

Sugarbear: I can't wait to see you

The words disappeared just as quickly as they appeared.

Sugarbear? JJ thought to herself. *I can't wait to see you?* She ran the words through her mind. She touched the phone to make sure she read it correctly.

"Hey baby. What are you doing here?" Bobby walked into his office.

She had so many emotions that she didn't know what to say. She wanted to slap that silly grin off his face.

"What's wrong?" he asked. Her facial expression gave her away.

"Who is Sugarbear?" Why is she saying that she can't wait to see you?"

Bobby smiled at her as he walked toward her. He tried to grab her hand, but she quickly pulled away.

"She's just a girl I was dating before you. She's no one." He glared into her eyes. His forehead furrowed.

"Before me? We've been dating almost a year," she accused. JJ folded her arms. "Why can't she wait to see you? It sounds like you two are still dating."

He inched closer to her and she inched further back.

"Every now and then, she still texts me. I agreed to meet up with her, but it was only to tell her that I'm with you now. I've tried telling her several times through text, but she's not getting the picture."

JJ was trying to decide if she believed him. She had only been to his house a few times and he didn't want anyone to know about their relationship, but he almost always answered her phone calls. He responded to her immediately by text if he was busy and would call back at the exact time that he said he would. But it was Monday, the day she normally went straight to her side of town to get to her yoga class. She felt dumb, thinking she had canceled yoga because she thought they'd celebrate his key with dinner after practice.

"Baby. You know how much I love you." He took another step toward her and she took another step back.

"Then tell Principal Rich that we're dating."

He dropped his head, sighing before looking back at her. "You have to let me do this in my own time."

"I think a year is enough."

"Baby, it's been more like nine months."

She was surprised that he was counting, but she wanted to stand firm. She needed to stand firm. She sighed. "I don't believe you." She shook her head before storming out of his office. Her heels echoed throughout the gym.

If he really wanted to prove that he loved her, he would have went straight to Principal Rich. He would have told his buddy, Deante. He wouldn't have kept her private. That's what she reminded herself over and over as she ignored his texts.

Now, she wished that she had responded. Maybe he was going to apologize before her favorite student attacked him. Maybe when he said he couldn't live without her, that was what he meant. Maybe he drugged himself. There were too many maybes. The way things were going, she would hide in her apartment forever sleeping on the love seat that reminded her so much of him.

13 UNDERGROUND NEWS

New Details in Deceased Coach Death
November 7th

Fannie Lou Hamer High School's varsity coach, Robert Charles Maker, also known as Coach Bobby, died Monday evening after a fight with one of his high school basketball players. It is not yet known if the cause of death is from the fight Maker had with his star player, Brodrick Timmons.

Timmons, a senior at Hamer High, is a popular prospect among the country's most impressive colleges. Timmons has yet to make a statement regarding the death of his coach. As of date, no one knows why he assaulted Maker.

Maker refused recommendations for medical treatment by both his colleague and first responders on the scene. Players admit that Maker seemed to be in great health after the fight, when practice was canceled.

Maker was known as a cool teacher, said students from Hamer High. He'd often let them "hang out at his ugly green and yellow house on Clydesdale Street." Students claim they'd party at Maker's house on school nights and weekends. Sometimes, students would even sleep over as he kept a spare key available to students at all times. School district representatives claimed that they were unaware of this information and are looking into the matter.

Stay tuned as Underground News always gives you the factual information first. While we work on this developing story, feel free to comment your thoughts below.

Deceased Coach Tried to Sabotage Player's Future
*November 15*th

Underground News has learned of new details in the case of Hamer High's recently deceased coach, Robert Charles Maker, also known as Coach Bobby. Witnesses say star player, Brodrick Timmons, had just learned that Maker tried to destroy his chance of receiving a full-ride scholarship to a prominent college in the NCAA program and even his chance of being drafted into the NBA. Witnesses believe the shock of this information could have caused Timmons to "lose it."

Timmons is currently free on bail from the assault case with now deceased coach, Maker. Maker's cause of death is still pending at this time. Stay tuned as Underground News always gives you the factual information first. While we work on this developing story, feel free to comment your thoughts below.

Deceased Coach Last Seen Alive By Secret Teacher Girlfriend
*November 18*th

Underground News has learned of new information regarding recently deceased coach, Robert Charles Maker, also known as Coach Bobby. While the public is still awaiting an official cause of death of Maker, Underground News has just received exclusive information regarding the case. Jameson Johnson, fellow teacher and secret lover of Maker, was the last person to see him alive on the night of his death. Friends close to Maker say Johnson had been stalking Maker for some time, even after he tried to break it off. It is stated that Maker could not be reached via phone immediately after Johnson left. Police declined to comment on these alarming details.

Stay tuned as Underground News always gives you the factual information first. While we work on this developing story, feel free to comment your thoughts below.

Deceased Coach Has Questionable Past
November 21st

While still awaiting official tox screen results, Underground News has learned of new information regarding recently deceased coach, Robert Charles Maker, also known as Coach Bobby. The sparsely attended funeral made friends question about Maker's past. Friends state that Hamer High's assistant varsity basketball coach, Deante Black, coordinated all services for the homegoing of the deceased. Black attempted to contact anyone in Maker's past, but was unsuccessful. No family members or friends from his previous place of residence attended Maker's homegoing services. It was like he didn't exist before.

Underground News looked into Maker's past and was able to determine that he lived in Mississippi two years ago, prior to moving to Texas. In Mississippi, he went by the alias, Rob. He lived in Florida four years earlier, prior to moving to Mississippi. In Florida, he went by the alias, Chuck. It was in Florida that Maker was accused of child molestation.

With no family, no prior friends, a secret lover and a mysterious death, only time will tell the true details of who Maker really was. Stay tuned as Underground News always gives you the factual information first. While we work on this developing story, feel free to comment your thoughts below.

14 JAMES TUCKER

James hated Bobby. Even though he knew that hate was a strong word, he still had those feelings. Even though he knew better than to speak ill of the dead, he still hated him. His wife was mourning the death of a lover that he supposedly didn't know about. How could she be so naïve, falling for a guy like Bobby? Sure, he drove a nice car, was super tall and had zero body fat, but his wife was too old to fall for favorable features. He was the man who provided for her.

It wasn't necessarily something that Bobby did, other than sleep with his wife, and it wasn't anything that he said. It was just him. He walked around like he was untouchable. Always smiling at the ladies and trying to one-up the guys. James hated him from the moment he met him.

His wife was throwing one of her unnecessary barbecues for the neighbors. She hosted those quarterly to make up for the fact that she had no real friends. James was standing in his normal spot, by the grill, talking to a few of his male neighbors. That's when he saw Bobby walk in. His wife was grinning ear to ear, taking him around to meet all of the ladies.

"Who in the hell is that?" His neighbor, Heath, noticed him as well.

All of the guys looked in Bobby's direction. The women were clearly flirting as if their husbands weren't fifty feet away.

James got his wife's attention. "Hey sweetheart, who's the new guest?"

Gloria ushered Bobby over toward the guys. She didn't even try to hide her excitement. "Honey, don't you remember? This is our new neighbor, Bobby."

James sized Bobby over. The other guys began to shake his hand while casually stating their names. Finally, Bobby's hand was extended to James. He looked at it for a second before finally accepting it.

"I'm Gloria's husband, James." James held a firm grip on Bobby a little longer than he should have. Bobby squeezed his hand harder and gave him a smirk, like he was in charge.

"Hey man, are you hungry?" Heath diverted Bobby's attention.

Bobby finally let his death grip go. James did all he could to not look pained by the aching bones in his hand.

"I wish I could." Bobby placed a hand on his stomach while glancing over the ribs, chicken and links on the grill. "But my boys and I are going to check out a game soon. Gloria wanted to make sure I met all of the neighbors, so I just stopped by."

Gloria? James thought. *How is he already on a first name basis with my wife?*

"Well at least have a beer." His other neighbor, Brock, motioned his half-empty bottle toward Bobby.

Bobby raised his hands up in surrender. "I don't drink, but thanks."

"Bobby is the varsity high school basketball coach at Hamer High," Gloria perked.

James wondered if the other guys thought she was smiling too much, then he looked over at the other guy's wives. They were smiling, too.

"Hamer High has a pretty good team. I heard they only lost two games last year," Heath explained.

"Well this year, they'll be undefeated." Bobby flashed his perfect smile. "I should be leaving, gentlemen, but I left a case of beer by the cooler." Bobby motioned near the patio, where the ladies emptied the box of beer.

"You can come by anytime," Tim added.

"I'll walk you out." Gloria smiled. She turned to walk away. James caught Bobby glance at her backside before nodding to the gentlemen, then following her out. James decided then and there that he didn't like that man.

James immediately became suspicious of Bobby. Where'd he come from? Why was he single? Why was he so cocky? It took him months to realize that he was hating on his neighbor.

"What is a grown man doing having kids over to his house like that anyway?" James peered through the kitchen window to see two high school boys walking into Coach Bobby's house.

"He's just giving the kids something safe to do," his wife answered while joining him in the kitchen.

"Don't they have their own homes to go to?" James fumed as he grabbed a beer from the fridge. He retired to his worn seat in front of the TV.

"You should really get to know him, Jim." His wife looked at him from the kitchen. "He really is a great guy."

James stopped his channel flipping to look at his wife. He couldn't believe she told her husband that the bachelor next door was a great guy. "You have a crush on him, don't you?" He accused.

Gloria looked offended. "No, you are just jealous of him."

"Jealous? Of a high school basketball teacher?"

"You didn't go to Heath or Tim's barbecues when you found out he'd be there. You've never said anything nice about him, and I don't think you've said two words to him since you met him."

It wasn't that he avoided his friends when they started inviting Bobby over, he had just gotten super busy. And he never had anything nice to say because there wasn't anything nice to say.

"I think you're reaching," he sighed before returning to the TV.

"Then prove it."

James finally found the fishing show that he was looking for. He set down the remote and picked up his beer.

Gloria stood directly in front of the TV and crossed her arms. "Prove it," she barked.

He hated when she did that. All he wanted to do in the evening was forget about his 10-hour shift. He needed to relax. He only had two hours before he had to get to bed so that he could do it all over again.

"What are you talking about, woman?" He took a sip from his beer.

"Bobby said that we could barbecue at his place Saturday morning. Why don't you come?"

"I have that fishing trip Saturday."

"You're fishing alone. You can go early, cut it short, then come over to Bobby's."

"Yea, okay. Just get out from in front of the TV."

After Gloria's third text, James finally left his fishing trip. He knew his wife and buddies were there, so he went straight over the Bobby's after parking his car in the garage.

Bobby had just opened his door to an awaiting woman with waist-length hair. James smirked, wondering what his wife would think if she saw this woman.

"I thought you said Saturday morning was a good time to come by?" James heard her say as he walked up behind her on the porch.

"I'm sorry, I'm having a few of my neighbors over." Bobby looked up at James, who was now standing beside the woman. He smiled nervously at James. "What's up, James? Come on in. Everyone's in the back."

James smiled at the woman. That's when he noticed that she wasn't a woman at all, but a girl. *She has to be no more than 15,* James thought. The heavy make-up suggested otherwise, but James knew better. His daughter tried that same trick when she was that age.

Bobby opened the door wider, suggesting that James go inside. So he did. James lingered behind the door to listen.

"I'm sorry, I have to go." Bobby closed the door on the girl. He looked startled to see James still standing there.

"Is that one of your students?"

"She is. I tutor her sometimes on Fridays, but I think she got the date wrong." Bobby casually walked past James. "It's just this way."

James didn't move. "That's odd. She didn't have any books. As a matter of fact, no paper or pen either. Nothing was in her hands."

"I have books here."

"You tutor kids alone in your house?" James remembered Bobby having groups of kids over all the time. Mostly, it was the basketball team using his home like a frat house, but he had never noticed him having students over alone.

Bobby appeared annoyed, but he flashed a quick smile. "Usually, the kids come over in groups. But kids will be kids."

James finally followed Bobby to the backyard. It seemed the entire street was there. "Man, everyone came out," James mumbled.

"You can blame your wife for that," Bobby confessed. He pulled a longneck from the cooler. "Here you go. Relax."

"Hey, Jimmy!" Both Heath and Tim gathered near him. Bobby casually strolled away from the group.

"Sorry I'm late, guys."

"We didn't expect you to show up. Everyone knows you're not that fond of Bobby," Heath joked.

James didn't know how to take that. He didn't think he was so obvious, until then. "Naw, it's not like that," James smiled. "He just seems a little suspicious to me."

Tim laughed. "What?"

"He always has these kids from the high school at his house and he just got here from who knows where? We don't know anything about him."

"It's been over a year now, James. He's their coach. I'm sure they have a relationship with him, just like we do."

"I just saw a little girl at his door. I'm just saying. I don't trust him." James took a sip from his bottle.

"He really is a cool guy, James. You need to lighten up."

James tried to lighten up. He refrained from saying anything that could even seem slightly negative about Bobby. He congratulated Bobby on his team's winning streak, turned an eye at the growing teen gatherings at his house, and actually smiled when his wife mentioned his name. He felt the same way he always had about him, but he just didn't want it to show.

His façade of liking Bobby came tumbling down when he realized that his wife talked to Bobby more than he had imagined. He normally fell asleep in front of the TV before finally getting up to go to the bed, but on his birthday, he decided to try something different.

His wife normally gave him special treatment for his birthday, so he wanted to be available to her as soon as she came out the shower. Once he heard the shower running, he snuck into their bedroom and began to pull back the covers. He went to the dresser to gather the clothes that he would soon change into. That's when he heard her phone buzz.

He looked over to the clock on the nightstand, then eyed her phone right next to it. *It's a little late,* James thought to himself.

He took the T-shirt in his hand over to the nightstand with him. The phone buzzed again.

He unlocked her phone to read the awaiting message.

Bobby: That's my favorite.

James didn't want to read anymore because he trusted his wife. Another message came through.

Bobby: □

James no longer tried to fight the urge. He clicked on the message to see the entire text stream.

Bobby: He'll probably like the pink one. Was the previous message.

James frantically scrolled up to see that she texted Bobby often. Most of the words that he could make out were about a barbecue here or a congratulations there. His wife consistently texted Bobby. The dates were going back to months. Maybe even a year. He was shocked.

He then heard the shower turn off. He put the phone back on the nightstand. He didn't notice anything on the texts to suggest that they were having a relationship, but they were clearly closer than he could imagine.

Maybe I'm overreacting, he thought. *But why would he send a winking emoji?* James was an old guy, but he knew winking was flirting. There were a lot of texts. He didn't even know his wife liked to text. He had never really seen her texting. She had to have been sneaking to text him. She texted more to Bobby than she said to James in a whole day.

James's heart sunk in his chest. He never thought his wife would cheat on him. Sure, he always thought she was too gorgeous for him, but he was her sole provider. He bought her everything she wanted. He was a nice enough husband.

He heard the bathroom door open. "Oh, honey. I was going to come to the living room to surprise you."

He tried to turn casually to face her, but his mouth dropped when he turned around. She wore a pink negligee.

James excused himself back into the living room. He needed time to think. He wanted to confront his wife, but he didn't want to lose her. They had been married twenty-five years and he never thought that something like this could happen. He took care of her completely. Why would she need to sleep with another man? He knew he needed dirt on Bobby. The guy was too sneaky to not have skeletons in his closet.

James's co-worker did private investigation work on the side. He got to work early the next morning to hire him.

"I'll get this information to you as soon as possible," his co-worker told him.

James had no clue that as soon as possible was two months, and the information he brought back wasn't alarming.

"Is this it?" James shook the single sheet of paper with Bobby's full name and previous address and place of employment."

"I told you to give me a little more time."

"I gave you two months."

"You can't rush these type of things. There's a lot that goes into finding people and making sure that the information I have is accurate."

"I paid you two months ago."

"I'll actually need another payment to continue my search."

James was angry. "You know what. I'll do this on my own."

James had forgotten all about doing his personal research until the night he saw his wife peeking out the window. He knew that she was spying on Bobby. That was the fuel he needed to begin his own search.

He pulled out the single sheet of paper that he left folded in the desk drawer in the family room. He was up late that night searching for several variations of Bobby's name. He'd finally found something so alarming, he knew it would give his wife pause. But he had stayed up so late that she was already asleep when he found it. He printed the article to give to her the next day. He'd tell her as soon as he came home from work. Those were his intentions, but that's not what happened.

"Baby, did you hear?" Gloria was sobbing at the door when he returned home.

"Hear what?" He had never seen her so upset before.

"Bobby's dead!"

James was shocked. There was no way he could tell his wife now. He felt sad for her. He tried to console her, until he saw that she was even obsessed with him in death. She spoke relentlessly to the paper and to the police about how much of a great guy Bobby was. He was sick of it.

One day, his wife answered a knock at the door.

"Hi ma'am. It's Chancellor again. From *Underground News*. I'm working on a follow-up story about Coach Bobby Maker. I'd like to ask you a few more questions, if that's alright."

Gloria started to cry at the sound of Bobby's name.

"Honey," James said as he ushered her away from the front door. "Why don't you go upstairs and get some rest. I'll talk to the reporter."

James watched as his wife slowly crept up the stairs. "One moment, sir." James left the reporter standing in his doorway.

He retrieved the single sheet of paper and story he printed about Bobby. He gave them both to the man. "This is all you need to know about Bobby."

The man read the printout aloud. "The *Davidsville Gazette*?" he read slowly.

"If you're a good journalist, you have all the information to help you find out who Bobby really was and I'll tell you, he wasn't no saint."

#accidentmurderer

15 DAVIDSVILLE GAZETTE

Coach Accused of Child Molestation

Police say a Davidsville, FL basketball coach allegedly molested one of his players. According to the police report, Chuck Maker was accused by a 10-year old from Hoop Dreams, a youth basketball skills organization, of "touching his privates."

The Davidsville Police Department said Maker alleged fondled the youth while they were alone one evening in May. The youth confided with another player a week after the alleged incident. It was that player who told Hoop Dreams director, who soon confirmed the suspected abuse with the alleged victim.

33 year-old Maker recently joined the Hoop Dreams Academy staff in January. In his role, he often counsels players and helps them with fundamentals of basketball. "This is simply a misunderstanding," Maker commented when being released with a $10,000 bond.

Hoop Dreams was founded in 1989 by Mitchell Rasby Sr. According to their website, "Hoop Dreams' mission is to foster the development of players on and off the court." It states that their staff is selected based on their moral character as well as their ability to motivate, teach and communicate with children.

Hoop Dreams current director is Mitchell Rasby Jr. Rasby has overseen the day-to-day activities of Hoop Dreams since his father retired five years before. "While we can't comment on specifics related to this matter because it is under active investigation, we can say that we are cooperating fully with authorities and are standing by to support their efforts," said Rasby. "To be clear, our organization is committed to adhering to all laws, policies and agreements – as evidenced by the fact that the individual charged in this case was arrested following our notification of authorities."

Maker is no longer employed at Hoop Dreams. Rasby did not state if this decision was policy driven or a personal choice. At this time, no trial has been set for this case.

16 CHARMAINE GRESHAM

Charmaine read the article with disgust. She somehow felt that a piece of the blame for the fiasco belonged her. She had her doubts about Bobby Maker, but she never seriously looked into them. Sure, this story wasn't a true news story, but a blog post. But people were taking it seriously. All of the students took it as real news and, most importantly, her boss did.

"These accusations are bold, Mrs. Gresham." Mr. Rich examined her carefully from the other side of his desk.

"I agree, but it's just a blog," she offered in her defense.

"Is it really just a blog?" Mr. Rich's chair squeaked as he leaned back. He crossed his leg and rested his hand on his chin. His eyes were lost on the ceiling in deep thought. Or perhaps, no thought at all.

Charmaine normally loved his patience, but today she hated it. He reminded her of her father. From his smooth gray hair to the blue circles around his pupils. There was an elephant in the room. She didn't know if she should acknowledge it or let him. She could be overreacting. Maybe there wasn't an elephant at all. Maybe the pressure of realizing that she was the one that vouched for this stranger to enter their school, be entrusted their students, and lead their biggest PR campaign, the basketball team, hadn't crossed his mind.

"This is the same *Underground News* that told us our mayor was embezzling money a year before the proof was unearthed," Mr. Rich said to the ceiling.

Charmaine shifted in her seat. She wasn't sure if the air was on in the small office or if the window was allowing in too much sun. Maybe she was having a hot flash.

"This is the same guy that exposed a student at Tubman High as one of the city's biggest drug dealers." Mr. Rich's eyes finally found Charmaine's.

She nodded haphazardly. "They have been known to uncover some pretty exclusive stories."

"Did you look into his past? How well did you know him?"

Parallel lines formed in Mr. Rich's forehead as his eyes slit in wonder. The question was valid, the elephant exposed.

Charmaine sighed. "I honestly didn't know him well, Mr. Rich."

Charmaine thought back to the simple recommendation. She casually mentioned to her brother in law that her friend, the previous basketball coach, was retiring soon. Not many knew that he was leaving and the job hadn't even been posted. Her brother-in-law knew a guy that was moving to the area. That was it. He knew a guy and she passed along his resume. She was helping a friend of a friend.

"I just knew that he was a basketball coach in Florida looking for a job in Texas. You guys seemed to hit it off so well. I figured that you did all the necessary background checks." If Charmaine was going to feel responsible for her part in Coach Bobby's hiring, Rich was going to accept his part of the responsibility, too.

"I didn't notice any red flags." Rich looked out the window. His gaze followed the flight of a mockingbird. It darted from an oak tree toward the tail of a fleeing squirrel. The bird attacked the squirrel twice before the squirrel found refuge underneath a parked car. "I don't like people shitting on my territory either."

Rich turned his seat around and faced Charmaine. "We need to get ahead of this thing, Mrs. Gresham. I hope none of these accusations are true, but I need to make sure my students are safe before the district gets involved. I need your help with that."

"Whatever you need, sir."

Rich and Charmaine agreed to call another assembly with the students. He addressed the students first, but she did most of the talking.

"Good afternoon, Hamer High. We are aware of the latest accusations against our late basketball coach, Bobby Maker. To reiterate what Mr. Rich has already explained, we have yet to receive validity of these accusations. And I know he's explained our policies surrounding issues such as these, but I'm here to address the services that you have available to you. We take these accusations seriously, and the safety of our students is our number one concern.

"Sexual abuse, assault and predators thrive in silence. If any of you feel like you have been a victim or are aware of any victims, please visit me. My evening office hours are still in effect. I am available to each of you whenever you need. If, for any reason, you don't feel comfortable speaking with me directly, please consult one of the counseling hotlines that have already been made available to you. If you need that information again, we have posted flyers in my office and several inconspicuous locations around the school.

"Victims of abuse often feel confused and guilty that the abuse has taken place. One may feel like they have the power to bury their feelings of doubt and want to seclude themselves from others. Sometimes, the effects of the abuse do not show until later in life but other times, you may feel an immediate distrust in everyone around you.

"Again, if you feel that you have been attacked or victimized for any small reason, even if you're unsure, please come talk to me or talk to someone. We don't want you to suffer in silence."

Charmaine glanced over the sea of students. She didn't want to focus on either of them because she didn't want either of them to feel singled out.

Over the course of the ten years that she had been a counselor at Hamer High, she had talked to her share of students with family problems. She knew that Rogue Grinstein's father was still in jail for a mortgage scam he participated in over a decade ago. His brother started selling drugs to help his mom with income. She had counseled his brother several times before he graduated to no avail. Although she had never counseled Rogue, he seemed to be doing well. His grades consistently improved and he was very active on the basketball team.

She also knew that Lisa Roundtree had been abused when she was in elementary school. She hadn't counseled her either. That information was in her school records. She was in district-sponsored therapy for a few years and as far as Charmaine could tell, it must have worked for her. She was talkative and giddy as any other teenage girl. Nothing stood out in her behavior.

Brodrick Timmon's mom had consulted with Charmaine a few years ago when looking for a dedicated therapist for her son. Broderick also seemed to be doing well, or so she thought, before he beat his coach to a bloody pulp. When the story came out about Coach Bobby spreading rumors to potential scouts about him, she knew that was just the trigger to reignite his anger issues.

"Look. I know you're trying to help the students, but the way you talked on stage made it sound like you really believe all that stuff they're saying about Coach Bobby." Deante was waiting for Charmaine in her office. She had hoped it would be available in case a student wanted to talk to her.

The tone in his voice prompted her to close her office door. She sat at her desk. "Deante, I know you two were very close, but this manner is serious. We can't afford to not take this seriously."

"Coach Bobby would give the shirt off his back if it could help one of these students. Now, you're asking if he abused them?"

Deante was emotional. He wasn't taking anything that had to do with Coach Bobby well. Rich had consulted Charmaine before asking Deante to take a leave of absence. It was clear to Charmaine that Deante didn't agree to the leave. He somehow felt compelled to fill Bobby's shoes, even though Mr. Rich was already looking for a replacement for Bobby's position.

"I simply asked if any student felt that they were a victim to come forth." Charmaine kept her voice low and her tone even. "In no way did I blame Bobby. Can't you see that I have the students' best interest in mind, too?"

"It doesn't feel like that, Mrs. Gresham." Deante's voice cracked. "It's bad enough that his killer is free. Now, you're asking his friends to add insult to injury by accusing a dead man?"

Charmaine wanted him out of her office. She knew no students would want to approach her with Deante around. Especially if this was his demeanor. "Can we continue this conversation later?"

Charmaine smiled, then stood. She walked past him to open the door. "I have a meeting soon and I need to prepare."

Deante huffed. He looked around the room for a few seconds and then finally stood. Charmaine opened the door for him to leave.

Charmaine didn't like how defensive Deante was regarding Bobby. She knew they had grown close, working together during the last two years, but she wondered if there was more to it. If Bobby really was a predator, Deante could be a victim of grooming.

Grooming wasn't a crime within itself, but it appeared that Bobby's charm went beyond a personal interest in JJ, had surpassed a guidance interest with students, and had also infiltrated his closest friends. The more people she talked to about Bobby, the more people thought he could do no wrong. Somehow, his charm made people overlook the possibility of him making a mistake.

She never got to know Bobby the way some of the other staff did. She tried her best to get to know him when he first came. "It's so great to finally meet you, Bobby. I'm Charmaine Gresham. I'm the one who forwarded your resume to Mr. Rich." It was the first day of mandatory staff training before the new school year began. Charmaine made a mental note to introduce herself once Rich told her he was hired.

Bobby bypassed her extended hand and wrapped his arms around her. "So, you're the one that I should thank. It's so great to finally meet you."

She was shocked. She didn't welcome any physical touching, but she didn't want to make him feel uncomfortable on his first day. She came from a family of huggers, so she learned how not to make a big deal out of it. But she'd have that conversation with him later.

When he finally let her go, she looked up into his beaming eyes. His grateful smile almost settled her uncomfortable feelings. Almost.

She took a deep breath. "Have you had a chance to meet everyone?" Charmaine introduced Bobby to half of the staff before training started. She noticed the mixed looks the new guy received from the other staff members when she took him around. But by the end of the training, all smirks spread into smiles. Bobby really knew how to work a room.

Charmaine never did have that talk with Bobby about unsolicited physical touch. Being a member of the teaching staff, she knew he'd get the message professionally in his annual training classes. Anyone that came into contact with students had to go through a background check. They had to attend necessary training about signs of abuse, dealing with abused youth, and reporting abuse. That's why she didn't understand why it was a difficult concept for Deante to grasp. Protect the students at all costs. He should know that.

17 PHIL MCMAHON

"Why didn't you tell me, Rob had a past?" Phil fumed. "I didn't know anything about his accusations."

"Who?" Jerry thought for a second. "Well, Chuck was never charged. It was only an accusation. And the guy that reported it isn't even a real reporter. You know that story came off a blog?" Jerry said.

"I don't know about no blog. That man said he was from a news station."

Phil remembered how happy Rob was when he scheduled the interview in Texas for the basketball position.

"I don't know how to thank you, Phil."

All Phil did was mention to a fellow church member that a friend from the basketball program he volunteered with was moving to Texas and looking for a job. He introduced the two to each other and a few weeks later, he was getting a thank-you.

Phil had always considered Rob a rolling stone, so he wasn't surprised the day he told him he was leaving.

"Well Phil, I think it's time for me to move on," Rob told him at the end of practice one day.

"What do you mean, son?" Phil was winded from his walk around the gym collecting basketballs. If his doctor didn't want him to stay active, he swore he'd sleep away his last days.

"As soon as I find me a job in Texas, I'm out of here. I just wanted to give you a heads up."

"Well, what you leaving for?" Phil leaned on the bleacher rail until his butt slid into the seat. "They ain't kicking you out the state, are they?"

Rob chuckled. "It's just time to move on. That's all. I want to thank you for all of your help you've given me over the years."

"Don't mention it, young buck."

Phil only had fond memories of Rob. Phil was a part of a non-profit sports program that gave inner city boys and girls something to do during the evening and weekends. He'd always said an idle mind was a devil's workshop.

Phil was once a schoolteacher, but spent the bulk of his years as a volunteer coach in basketball, football, baseball and soccer. He'd coach kids from grade school to high school. He coached his two boys and two girls when they were younger, and he was beginning to coach his grandkids until he realized that standing outside for long periods of time wasn't ideal for his ailing health. He retired to catching up on the TV shows he had missed all those years, until his daughter suggested he work at SportNation Skills camp.

"Oh I don't know, honey. You know my knees are bad."

"Dad. They have an office position and it's all indoor. You'll do great," his daughter, Margie, convinced him.

He always told her that she convinced him, but it didn't take long for him to grow tired of watching reruns. The job didn't pay well, but he didn't do it for the pay.

Rob started a year after he did and he took him under his wing. Rob worked with the 10-12 year old boys and girls. His group was a rotating group, meaning they'd spend a week at a time on any given sport before selecting one that they'd focus on. Phil remembered Rob bringing the youth snacks and making jokes with them. Kids would stay in Rob's group longer just because they liked Rob so much. A lot of the kids didn't have active fathers in their lives, so SportNation became a truly integral family to them.

"The boy that accused him was about 10 years old," Jerry said.

"You know he worked with kids around the same age here. Both boys and girls. And I remember the kids just loving him. Some would stay in his group as long as they could because they looked up to him so much. Seems if he had a problem with kids, we'd know about it. Do you think the boy made it up?"

"I don't know. It was just a fiasco. Said Chuck touched him wrong."

"You think the boy may have been confused?"

"That's what I reckoned because they didn't bring no charges to him. I always knew him as a good guy, too."

Phil was shocked to hear that a promising young coach was being accused of horrendous acts. He was saddened even more to learn that the accusations only came after his death. "That's sad. The man can't even rest in peace without people spitting on his name," Phil churned.

"I would have liked to have attended the funeral," Jerry confessed.

"Yea, me too. But I can't move around much anyhow with this Arthur in my knees."

"It's good to talk to you, you hear? Even if I don't like the circumstances."

"Alright, old man. Hit me up sometime, why don't you? Ain't no telling how many more good years I got left in me." Phil hung up the phone.

"Daddy, you lying about Rob?" Margie called to Phil as soon as he clicked end.

"What you talkin' bout, gul? Calling me out my name."

"You thought Rob decided to leave on his own?"

"What you mean?"

"I thought I told you Tiffany said she'd report him if he didn't quit. She said he was saying inappropriate things to her daughter."

18 JEREMY CAMBRIDGE

Jerry hung up with Phil feeling a little unnerved about what he had heard about Chuck. Like Phil, he didn't think it was fair to talk about a man's supposed transgressions after his death, but this issue brought back memories.

Jerry should have known when that guy called him the week before.

"Uhm. Yes. I'm calling for Jeremy Cambridge," a soft voice crawled through the phone.

Jerry didn't know if it was a woman or a kid, but no one called him Jeremy except bill collectors. "You got the wrong number."

"No, I'm pretty sure it's the right number," the voice accused. "Jeremy Cambridge of Harlandale Road? Friend of child molester, Robert Charles Maker? I think you called him Chuck."

"Wait just a damn minute. You got some nerve."

"I'm not trying to upset you, I just wanted to follow-up on the story."

"What story? Who is this?"

"Chancellor of *Underground News*. I just learned of a Davidsville Gazette story where you commented that Chuck appeared to be a model citizen and that maybe the kid was confused."

Jerry didn't like the boy's questioning. He sounded a bit accusatory. Jerry didn't even know if he had made those statements. He remembered a few people asking him about Chuck when that boy accused him of touching him, but he couldn't recall what he said.

"I just want to ask you a few more questions, if that's okay," the boy squeaked through the phone.

"No, you may not. If you say you got some quote from me, use that." Jerry hung up the phone.

Jerry didn't think Chuck had done anything to that boy. It wasn't that he thought the boy was lying. Kids just got a little puzzled sometimes. Jerry had worked beside Chuck for a few years and he was practically a saint. Chuck's personal life seemed to be a mess with him dating so many women, but he was great with the kids.

"I think that's the fifth girl I done seen to come visit you this year," he told Chuck while at work one day.

"What can I say? Ladies love cool Chuck," Chuck chuckled.

"Who you date is your business, but I'm saying, if I noticed, I'm sure others have too. You don't want to create a reputation of instability."

Jerry could tell that Chuck didn't like his statement. He tried to make it sound as non-judgmental as he could. Jerry smiled at him. He realized that he was telling a grown man about his dating habits.

"How do you know those aren't my sisters? Or my cousins?" Chuck's smile was gone. His cool expression matched his even tone.

Jerry eyed the young girl smiling at Chuck from across the room. She raised the weighted plastic bag that she held. She had brought him lunch. Her seductive smile, short skirt, and low top was enough proof for him. The girls would often bring him lunch or meet him out front after work.

Chuck winked at the girl before making eye contact with Jerry. "You're right. Thanks for the insight. I'll take your advice." Chuck jogged over to meet the girl and ushered her into his office.

In addition to being a great coach, Chuck was coachable. Jerry never remembered seeing another girl stop by to see Chuck again. Chuck was about two decades his junior and respected Jerry like a father figure.

Jerry was sure that Chuck's biggest mistake was allowing himself to be alone with any of the kids. The allegations came weeks after the incident was supposed to have occurred. Mitch, the program director, called Jerry into his office.

"Were you here on March second?" Mitch asked urgently.

162

Jerry took a seat. He couldn't even remember what he had done the day before, let alone two weeks ago. "What day was that?"

"It was a Tuesday. Were you here then? You usually work late with Chuck, don't you?"

"I haven't missed any days, so I'm sure I was. Why? What's this about?"

"Cameron Braswell has stated that Chuck touched him inappropriately. That…" Mitch cleared his throat. "He requested Cameron to touch him inappropriately."

"What?" Jerry's mind raced. He tried to recall anything he could from that day. Every day seemed almost the same. There was a day that Cameron didn't come after school. He didn't come for two whole days. As a matter of fact, Jerry hadn't seen him in a while. Mitch was still expecting an answer. "I really can't remember anything happening that day. Nothing that stands out."

"Well, we've had to suspend Chuck."

"Wait, what? Suspend him for what?"

"Our policy states that an adult should never be alone with a child. Chuck did agree that he was alone with Cameron."

"Did he say he did something to him?"

"The police will likely need to speak with you. You two are the only ones I had on staff during the time of the incident."

Jerry remembered that day. He remembered that he was about to lock up when he saw that Chuck was still in the building.

"Hey, man. I almost locked you in. What are you still doing here?"

"Cameron's mom was late picking him up again. I just walked him out."

Jerry looked at his watch. "We need to talk to her about that. That boy should have been picked up an hour ago."

Chuck shrugged. "Single mothers."

Jerry and Chuck left the building at the same time. Something like that had happened before, but it was nothing out of the ordinary.

"Mitch. I remember that day. Cameron's mom picked him up late. She's always picking him up late."

Mitch sighed. "I know, but Chuck still shouldn't have been alone with Cameron."

"Do you think he really did something to that kid? Come on, Mitch. You know how much Chuck does for these kids. He'd give them the shirt off his back."

"That may be true, Jerry, but we have to follow protocol. Things like this wouldn't happen if he had just followed protocol. I'll alert the rest of the staff of Chuck's suspension. Please, keep the details between us for now."

Jerry called Chuck as soon as he left Mitch's office. He tried to get out of earshot of the kids. "Mitch just told me about your suspension Chuck."

"Yea, he stopped me as soon as I walked into the building this morning. That's what happens when you don't follow the rules."

"What happened?"

"I found Cameron in the bathroom. I didn't even know he was in there. I thought all of the kids had left. I think I spooked him because I was surprised about him being there. Anyway, I told him we could go call his mom again, but he just decided to wait out front. I walked him out and that's when I saw you."

"So, it was just a big misunderstanding?" Jerry knew there was an explanation for this. "If we just explain to Mitch-"

"No, Mitch is right. When I saw him in the bathroom, I should have just walked out. I should have come and got you so that we could both walk him outside. That's where I failed."

"There's no way you could have known. Cameron is such a shy kid. I can't believe he'd accuse you of something like that."

"Maybe he just got confused. You know how kids are."

Jerry couldn't believe how calm Chuck was. He was always thinking about the kids and never about himself. The police, the newspaper, and even the Hoop Dreams harassed Chuck for weeks until finally the charges were dropped. Jerry never did see Cameron again, but he met up with Chuck a few times for lunch.

"How are you holding on, Chuck?" He treated Chuck to his favorite seafood restaurant.

"I'm doing okay, man. I'm happy they finally got the charges dropped, but I still feel bad about everything that has happened."

"What do you feel bad for? You didn't even do anything."

"Just to be accused of something like that. I'm really thinking about moving on. Getting a fresh start."

"I think a fresh start would be great for you. I have a buddy in Mississippi. He runs a program similar to ours and they're always hiring. I can put a word in, if you're interested."

"I appreciate it, Jerry."

Jerry didn't hear anything else about the ordeal until that newsperson called him out the blue. Then Phil called him a few days later to tell him that Chuck was dead.

Jerry dialed his nephew. He had been at Hoop Dreams when the incident happened. He looked up to Chuck.

"Hey, nephew."

"What's up, Unc!"

"I called to tell you some bad news."

"Really?" Eshon's voice turned solemn. "What happened?"

"Remember Chuck. He used to work at Hoop Dreams."

"You talking about the guy that molested Cameron?"

"He was accused of molesting-"

"I forgot that you were real cool with him. What happened to him?" Eshon's solemn voice was now apathetic.

"He died. It happened about..."

"That's what-" Eshon interrupted his uncle, but then stopped. "I'm sorry to hear that, Unc. Hopefully, Cameron will have some peace."

"What?"

"Sorry, Unc. My mom's calling me. You know how she gets if she has to say my name more than once. I love you." Eshon hung up the phone.

Jerry couldn't believe how disrespectful his nephew was. It seemed like no one respected the dead anymore.

19 ESHON BARNETT

Eshon couldn't believe his uncle. He had the nerve to call him looking for sympathy because a pedophile had died. Eshon knew that Chuck had violated Cameron. That's why he reported it.

Cameron didn't come to Hoop Dreams the day after it happened. He didn't come the day after that either. Eshon saw him at school the next day and asked him why.

"Hey, man! Where have you been?" Eshon walked up to Cameron after spotting him sitting by himself underneath the tree farthest from the playground.

Eshon and Cameron had different teachers, but they were both in the fifth grade. They often played basketball together during recess after lunch.

"I've been around," Cameron mumbled. He stared at his fumbling hands that sat in his lap. Eshon knew something wasn't right with him.

"You want to play some ball?"

Cameron just shook his head. Eshon stared at him for a few minutes. Cameron didn't talk a lot, but he liked to play. Even when he got in trouble really bad at home and was on punishment for a week, he still played. Even when their mean teacher told him that she didn't think he was smart enough to work for the FBI, he still played. Even when he said his lights were off at home and his mom didn't give him lunch money, he still played. Eshon didn't know why Cameron didn't want to play, but he decided to leave him alone.

It took another two days for Eshon's curiosity to get the best of him. He found Cameron sitting under that same tree at recess.

"Hey, Cameron. Are you going to come to Hoop Dreams today?"

Cameron just shook his head. He still didn't make eye contact with Eshon. Eshon sat next to Cameron so that he could look him in the eyes.

"What's wrong, Cameron? Why don't you want to play with me?"

"I just don't want to."

"What happened? The last time I saw you playing was at Hoop Dreams last week."

"My mom said I don't have to go if I don't want to."

"I thought your mom worked in the evening. I thought you liked to get the snacks they have at Hoop Dreams. I saved my apple slices for you, but you never came." Eshon didn't like fruit as much as Cameron did. Eshon offering his apple slices was how they became friends. Everyone used to think that Cameron was mean because he was quiet and so big, but they all soon found out that he was harmless.

"I'm not going back there."

"Back where?" Cameron wouldn't even look up at Eshon.

"Just leave me alone. Okay?"

"Okay." Eshon stood up. "I'm just going to ask everyone at Hoop Dreams why you're not coming. I'm going to ask Uncle Jerry, Mr. Mitch, Mr. Chuck."

"Noooo," Cameron wailed at the mention of Mr. Chuck's name.

Cameron stared up at Eshon. His face was angry, but his eyes looked scared. Eshon sat back down next to Cameron.

"What happened, Cameron? You can tell me."

"I just don't like Hoop Dreams." Cameron crossed his arms and stared at his legs.

"Yes you do. You always said that you liked it. Remember, you said you would work there one day since you probably wouldn't work for the FBI."

"No. I don't care what I said."

"Something happened, didn't it?" Eshon spoke barely above a whisper. It didn't matter because no one was close enough to even hear them talk.

"I don't want to talk about it."

"Something happened with Mr. Chuck, didn't it?"

"I said I don't want to talk about it." Cameron was crying now. He tried wiping his eyes, but he couldn't wipe them fast enough. Eshon was scared because he didn't know what to do.

"You can tell me, Cameron. Tell me what happened."

"I can't. I'm not telling nobody." Cameron got up and ran back inside the building.

Eshon stood underneath the tree confused. It must have been something bad if it made Cameron cry. He didn't even cry when the kids made fun of his mom's beat up car. He didn't know what to do, but he knew he didn't want Cameron to be so scared. He didn't think he should be so alone. Eshon wanted to help, but he didn't know how.

Eshon couldn't get his mind off of how angry and scared Cameron was. He sat in class listening to his teacher explain math problems on the board. He didn't hear a word she said but before he knew it, his hand was raised.

"Do you know the answer, Eshon?" his teacher asked.

"Huh?" Eshon thought for a second before shaking his head. "No. How can you help your friend if they say they don't want help?"

His teacher was puzzled. "With math problems?" she asked. "Are you paying attention, Eshon?"

He sighed. "Nevermind."

Eshon sat at the dining table for hours looking at his math book, but not seeing a thing on the page. *Why would he stop coming to Hoop Dreams?*

"Don't make me call you again!" His mom's tone demanded his attention.

"Mama, my friend don't want to play with me at school and he stopped coming to Hoop Dreams. What should I do?"

"It sounds like your friend found some new friends. Now, how long is it gone take you to finish that homework?"

Eshon tried to forget it. Maybe his mom was right. Maybe Cameron would get over it and find some new friends. Eshon tried to hang out with his other friends at recess, but he couldn't shake the chills that he got when Cameron screamed at him. He looked over to the tree to find Cameron. He wasn't there.

Eshon left the middle of his soccer game to find Cameron's teacher. "Mrs. James, where's Cameron?"

"He's not in today, sweetie. He may be home sick."

Eshon was scared. He spent days thinking about helping his friend, but he didn't do anything. And now, he may be gone forever. "Are you sure?"

"I haven't talked with him, sweetie. Hopefully he'll be back on Monday."

Eshon was angry. He couldn't believe he missed the chance to help his friend. He wanted to rush right over to Mr. Chuck when he saw him laughing with some of the other kids while playing basketball. He was halfway there when he stopped in his tracks. *If the thought of Mr. Chuck made Cameron that afraid when he wasn't even there, what will he do to me?*

Cameron turned around and found his uncle.

"Uncle Jerry, I need to talk to you."

His uncle was showing one of the big kids the proper dribbling technique, something the kid should have already known at his age, so Eshon didn't think that was important. "It's really important, Uncle."

Uncle Jerry excused himself from the big kid to talk to Eshon. "What's up, nephew?"

"If a grown up does something to make a kid cry, what should that kid do?"

His uncle looked confused. He tried to elaborate. "I mean, if the kid doesn't tell, but if their friend knows that the grown up made him

173

cry, is there something you think his friend should do?"

"What's going on, Eshon? Is there something else you need to tell me?"

"No, Uncle. I am telling you. What do you do if a grown-up makes a kid cry? I mean, grown-ups don't really get in trouble for that type of thing. You can't tell on a grown-up, right?"

"You can always tell, Eshon. You can tell a grown-up you trust. Like me." Uncle Jerry looked at Eshon knowingly. "Is there something you want to tell me?"

"No, I'm just trying to help a friend…" Eshon didn't want to betray Cameron, but he didn't want his uncle putting two and two together. "From school. My friends were talking about a grown-up making a kid cry."

"Like a teacher?" his uncle asked.

"Yea." Eshon didn't know why he didn't think of that. "Like a teacher. How can you tell on a teacher?"

"You know teachers have bosses that they report to. You could always tell the principal. Actually, you should tell a parent and let them tell the principal if the teacher is making the kid cry."

"That's good advice, Uncle. Thank you." Eshon smiled. He began to walk away. *So, you can tell on adults.*

"Eshon!" He turned around to face his uncle. "If there's something going on with you, you know you can trust me, right?"

"I know, Unc." Eshon smiled and returned to his own class. He thought over and over about who to tell. If the teacher worked for the principal, who does Mr. Chuck work for?

Mr. Mitch walked into his classroom right before he did. "Don't forget we have a meeting after all the kids leave," Mitch told Eshon's teacher.

That's it. Mitch is over all of the teachers at Hoop Dreams.

"Can I talk to you, Mr. Mitch?" Eshon whispered, "In private?"

Mr. Mitch led Eshon to his office right away. Eshon stood by the door, hoping that his uncle couldn't see him through the large glass windows from the gym.

"How may I help you, Eshon?"

"Is it true that you're over all of the teachers here?"

Mr. Mitch looked concerned. He answered slowly, "Yes."

"I think one of the teachers did something to Cameron. That's why he won't come back, but he won't tell me what happened. He just cried and told me not to say anything. But then he didn't come to school today and I'm scared he could be hurt. And I don't want to get in trouble for telling you. But I don't want something to happen to him and I didn't do anything about it. You always say that safety is our first concern, but I don't think Cameron is safe. I don't think he felt safe here and that's why he's gone." Eshon let it all out in one breath. He probably should have made sure it was safe to tell Mr. Mitch, but he couldn't hold it in anymore.

"Did he say who or what happened to him?" Mr. Mitch said slowly. It appeared to Eshon that he took him seriously, but he was still afraid of getting in trouble.

Eshon glanced out of the window. He still saw the big kids playing with his uncle. No one seemed to be looking his way. "I think it was Mr. Chuck," Eshon whispered. "He screamed and looked really scared when I said his name. He got really mad at me for saying his name."

Mr. Mitch took in a deep breath. He stared at his computer. Eshon didn't know why, because the computer wasn't even on. Eshon was afraid that he wasn't going to take him seriously. "Please, Mr. Mitch. Can you just make sure he's okay? I'm sure you have his phone number. Please don't tell him I said anything. I just want to make sure he's okay, and I don't want him to be scared anymore. I have to go. I don't want anyone to know I told."

Mr. Mitch nodded to Eshon. "Thank you, Eshon. I will make sure he is okay. I'm happy that you care about your friend like that. I'll make sure that he's safe. You have my word."

Eshon smiled. He felt like a huge burden was lifted off his shoulders. If something bad happened, Mr. Mitch would fix it. If nothing bad happened, Mr. Mitch wouldn't say that it was him.

Eshon had almost forgotten how worried he was about Cameron, until he saw him sitting underneath that tree again during recess. He was nervous about approaching him, but needed to know if anything he told Mr. Mitch had helped.

"Hey. Cameron. Were you sick Friday?"

Cameron glanced up at Eshon, then stared back out into the street. "I skipped school."

"Really? And your mom let you?"

"Naw. She found out. That's why I'm here today."

Cameron didn't seem too happy, but he didn't seem as upset as he had the week before. Eshon liked that he at least talked to him. "Wanna play ball?"

Cameron looked back at Eshon. He spoke through a slow smirk, "maybe tomorrow."

Eshon smiled. "Okay. We'll play tomorrow."

But Eshon didn't play with Cameron the next day or any day after that. He found out by hearsay of his uncle that Mr. Chuck was suspended, and he knew exactly why.

It wasn't until the police and the reporters came around that Eshon knew what had happened to Cameron. Everyone thought Cameron was a liar, but no one saw his face that day. Eshon knew that whatever Cameron was scared of, it was real. And if Mr. Chuck could make Cameron that scared, he could do it to any other kid at Hoop Dreams, too.

Eshon never knew what happened to Cameron after that. One of his classmates said he had moved. Eshon was never sure if he had helped Cameron or hurt him, but he didn't regret telling Mitch. He never wanted to see someone look the way that Cameron did that day. He never wanted to feel like Cameron did that day either. To him, what he did was right and he'd never feel guilty about it.

20 CAMERON BRASWELL

"Good game, Cam." Coach Black patted Cameron on the back. "We're going to have to work on that jump shot in practice this week. But you're doing good to not have touched a ball in a while."

"Thanks, Coach." Cameron wasn't starting, but he was happy to be a part of the team. To be a part of something without people looking at him funny.

"Great job, Cam." Lisa winked at him on her way across the gym. Cameron hurried out the back because he didn't want people seeing that his mom was picking him up.

"You know I can drive, Mom," he said as he slid into the passenger seat.

"Not my car, you can't."

Cameron didn't want to start a new argument with her. She wasn't one to back down and she hardly ever saw things his way. It was her idea that he try to join the basketball team, but it was clear that if he wanted a car, he'd need to work instead.

"You seem to be fitting in nicely." His mom glanced over at him and smiled.

Cameron smiled back at her. He didn't know if he was fitting in well or not. They guys were nice to him, but it wasn't like they were asking him hang out with them. He could probably ask them if he could join, but he didn't want to sound like a dork. He had problems fitting in at the last school.

Cameron had fit in nicely with the girls. He dated almost all of them. That was mostly why the guys didn't like him. How was he to know which girl belonged to who? The guys didn't say it was because he dated their girls, but why else would they plot to jump him? Between the trouble he'd get into with the guys and the STD he caught by sleeping around, his mom thought it was time for a change. Cameron was happy for change. He didn't like it there anyway.

Cameron was depressed. He tried telling his mom that, but she didn't take him seriously.

"Last week, it was Kiesha; this week it's Johnnique. It's no wonder you caught this disease. You keep on and you'll catch something that you can't get cured." She scolded him right in front of the doctor.

He hated that he had to tell her, but the pain got so severe that he just had to go to the doctor. If his mom wasn't so overprotective, he could have tried to go alone, but she wouldn't have it. She had been taking him to Dr. Kem since they moved to Texas six years before.

"I don't see you very often, Cameron, but it seems like something else may be going on. Is there anything else you want to talk about?"

Cameron just shook his head.

"I know this isn't the greatest news, but some penicillin will clear it right up. If what your mom says is right, you could have an overactive sex drive. You could have an addiction. And you seem a bit unhappy. Do you think it's possible that you may be a little depressed?"

Cameron looked up at Dr. Kem. He could be right. He felt horrible all the time. He didn't know that it was depression, but he knew that depressed people were often sad. At first, the thrill of getting with a new girl excited him, but it wasn't exciting anymore. Especially when one of the guys yelled down the hallway that he was infecting the entire student body.

"My baby ain't depressed. He's ashamed."

"Ms. Braswell. I could refer him to another doctor who specializes in this sort of thing. She could talk to him and make a determination. It could help him in the long run. What do you think about that, Cameron?"

Dr. Kem looked at Cameron. Cameron looked at his mom.

"Just write us the prescription and we can go."

Cameron tried to bring up the conversation again with his mom that evening. If Dr. Kem said this lady could help him, then maybe he should get some help.

"Can we just talk to her, Mom? I do feel sad all the time."

"You don't have anything to be sad about, son. You have all those friends. You're always on that phone. You're very popular. Your grades could be better, but they're alright."

"I don't know. I just feel like-"

"You don't know, Cameron, but I'm telling you. If you let those people in your head, they can have you believing all sorts of things. Just stop it with all the girls. Find you one nice girl you like, if you got to be out there like that."

Cameron wanted to think that she was right, but he knew better. She just didn't want to pay for it. Cameron was sure that his mom complained about money since the day he was born. He had never met his dad, but that's probably what ran him off.

"Honey, do you really think you need to keep talking to those doctors? Each visit costs me $100. They said they'd give me a discount, but if I still owe $100, what kind of discount is that?"

Cameron was ten then. The detective referred them to a therapist. She specialized in child molestation cases.

Cameron just shrugged. He didn't know if talking with the lady was helping or not, but he did like her. She didn't make him feel like he made the story up. She didn't tell him that he may have been confused.

"I tell you what, baby." His mom grabbed him by both shoulders and looked him in the eyes. "We're going to move to Texas. My mom and siblings are there. You can meet your cousins. Start a new school. We can just get away from this whole thing. What do you think about that?"

"I guess," Cameron uttered.

That was that. His mom told the detectives that they would no longer cooperate in the case. That regardless of whether Cameron was confused or not, the case wasn't going to help him. Cameron knew that she was right. He didn't know how Mr. Mitch found out anyway. He didn't even want to tell Mr. Mitch, but he said that he would help.

"Thank you for joining me, Ms. Braswell." Mr. Mitch shook his mom's hand. "Cameron." Mr. Mitch shook Cameron's hand. "Please, have a seat."

Mr. Mitch talked to him like he knew everything. He said there was an incident that happened between him and Mr. Chuck and he didn't want Cameron to feel unsafe. That he was there to make sure if anyone had done anything wrong that they would be punished. Cameron wasn't going to say anything, but his mom made him. She made him tell the whole story to her and Mr. Mitch.

His mom gasped. She covered her mouth with tear-filled eyes when he said it, when he said that Mr. Chuck came in while he was standing at the urinal, that he knew it was him when he massaged his shoulders from behind. That he told him not to zip his pants just yet. That he touched him and said that it was normal. That he pulled down his shorts a little to ask Cameron to touch him, too.

"Why Cam? Why did you let him-"

Mr. Mitch interrupted his mom. "This should have never happened Cameron. Mr. Chuck should have never walked in the bathroom alone with you."

Cameron heard Mr. Mitch, but he couldn't stop looking into his mom's eyes. Her eyes told him that it was his fault. Her face said that he was a disgrace. Tears began to flow from his own eyes. "That's why I didn't want to tell. I should have walked out of the bathroom. I should have waited until I got home to pee."

"You didn't do anything wrong, Cameron," he heard Mr. Mitch say.

"I'm sorry, Mama," Cameron pleaded to his mom. He stood because he wanted to hug her, but she stood up too.

"Ms. Braswell, please remain seated. I need to discuss protocol with you. We really want to keep all of our children safe. We do not tolerate this type of behavior. Mr. Chuck will be suspended immediately and I have to report this to the police."

His mom looked around the room. Just like Cameron, she seemed to be looking for a way to escape. She had to be disappointed in him.

Maybe if Cameron hadn't let Mr. Mitch massage his shoulders before, he wouldn't have come into the bathroom. Maybe he shouldn't have come to Hoop Dreams in the first place. His mom chose to send him there. She said he needed to do something after school instead of running up her light bill and eating all of her food. She was the one who picked him up late. If she didn't pick him up late, Mr. Chuck wouldn't have found him alone in the bathroom.

Those thoughts ran through Cameron's mind almost every day. Almost every day that year, he changed his mind of who to be mad at. He hated his mom for taking him to that place and not picking him up on time. He hated his father for never meeting him. A father who could have protected him against a big man like Mr. Chuck. He hated Mr. Mitch for hiring Mr. Chuck. He hated the police officers and the counselor who said they'd help, but they never made him feel better. Once he moved to Texas, he hated Florida. He even stopped drinking orange juice.

He decided he'd be a new person in the new state. He and his mom moved in with his grandma, so there was always someone there. By the time he made it to middle school, his cousin taught him how to talk to girls. He made the prettiest, most popular girl his girlfriend and that made everyone respect him.

He did everything the girl wanted, but eventually she dumped him. Somehow, that brought back every bad memory he ever had. He didn't want to lose people's respect. What if they thought he was as weak as he felt?

He was bigger. He was stronger. He wasn't that little ten-year old boy that let some grown man tell him what to do. His girlfriend wouldn't decide how popular he had to be. He was going to be his own man. He vowed then that his girlfriend would wish she was still with him because every girl would want him. He was going to be the most popular and the coolest kid wherever he went. No one would make him feel less than ever again. And if he ever saw Mr. Chuck again, he would kill him.

Pretty soon, he had all the girls. Everyone said he was the man. He always dumped the girls first because he would never be dumped again. He walked around like he was the man, even if he didn't actually feel that way. He once tried basketball again, but when the coach wouldn't let him start, he quit.

Catching that disease made him think twice. It helped him realize that he wasn't as powerful as he thought he was. And if the boys at school jumped him like they said they would, he knew he'd be the laughing stock of the town. He skipped school and avoided his classmates as much as he could. He didn't know how long he could keep it up, but he'd try. One day, he found out that he didn't have to try anymore.

"Guess what, y'all? I got the job!" his mom yelled to Cameron and his grandmother, interrupting their TV show.

"Congratulations," Cameron tried to sound happy, but he didn't have it in him.

"We'll finally get out of your hair, Momma. The job is in the suburbs.

How do you feel about moving, Cameron?"

Cameron smiled. This may be good news after all. Cameron could reinvent himself. Although the new city was only half an hour away, he would be in a whole new school district. His reputation wouldn't precede him there. He could reinvent himself again. This time, he wouldn't date all the girls. He'd try to do a better job of making friends. He wouldn't try so hard to be cool. Maybe he could settle for being a second-string basketball player. This move could be just what he needed.

The week before school started, his mom drove him all around the school and the neighborhood so that it would feel familiar. The school was nestled in the middle of a middle class neighborhood. He learned the route of the public transportation bus, where the closest fast food joints were, and the closest grocery store. He hated that he didn't have a car, but he was comfortable with his new surroundings. His bus route was only a ten-minute ride from their apartments.

Cameron tried to chipper up for his first day. He practiced correcting his posture and tried making eye contact in the hallway. A few girls smiled at him. Determined to stay focused this time, he smiled back and kept walking. When he first met Mike, he thought he was on the right track. Mike was inviting and made him feel that he might have a chance at joining the basketball team. Things were moving nicely, until Mike opened the gym doors.

The very thing he had run from all of those years was standing before him. He couldn't believe it. Mr. Chuck looked exactly the same. His fear paralyzed him. Cameron realized that he could never run from his problems. He would never get away from the pain. This world wasn't created for him. There was only suffering here. He needed to get away.

Cameron barely realized all the players that ran toward Mr. Chuck. They were separating a fight. He wanted to leave the gym, but thought the other players had already saw how scared he was. It took every bit of energy he had to show some type of confidence. He would then find a reason to leave. He saw a few players picking up things that fell on the floor, so he blended in with them.

The boy he came to know as Brodrick was yelling. He was angry. Cameron slipped out the back door of the gym while the other players helped Mr. Chuck clean his face. He didn't know what to do, but he knew he couldn't stay there.

Cameron walked past the parked cars and made it to the corner before realizing that he had someone's keys in his hand. He turned around to return the keys, then noticed the Charger he stood next to. He looked at the keys, then back at the Charger. He pushed the lock button on the Dodge key fob, almost shocked to hear the car chirp. The back door to the gym opened. Cameron didn't know why, but he hid on the side of the building.

Mr. Chuck's face was bloody. Cameron didn't know what happened, but he knew that whatever it was, Mr. Chuck deserved it. Cameron waited for Brodrick to ride away in the squad car. He heard a short skinny man ask the players if they needed something. Cameron knew what he meant by *something*.

Cameron wasn't into drugs, but he thought a new hobby wouldn't be such a bad idea. He'd need something to help him get away from the new life that unexpectedly turned into a mirror of his old life. He tried, but he wasn't strong enough to get over it. He felt too weak.

Cameron caught up with the short guy after he turned the corner. "Hey, what's up man?"

The short guy looked him up and down. He must have realized that he wasn't a threat. "You trying to get high?"

"I don't know. I guess. I don't have a lot of money. What do you suggest?"

"That depends on how high you want to get?"

"I don't know. I just got a lot of drama. I need to get away from it all. Just-" Cameron realized that drugs probably weren't the best idea. Maybe he could run away. He was old enough to find a job somewhere. He could just drop out of school.

"I got just the thing. These pills will get you there. I'm only going to charge you for two, but I'll give you four. Then, if you like it, you know where to find me."

Cameron was confused. He didn't know where to find him. It was his first time even at the school. "I don't know, man."

"I feel your hesitation. I get it. But I really want to win your trust, so I'll sell you one and give you three for free. You won't find a better deal."

"What is it?"

"It's China Wh-… well, fentanyl man. I'm telling you, you'll enjoy these. They'll get you right."

The short guy pulled a small bag out of his pocket. Cameron just looked at it. The man nodded toward him impatiently while looking up and down the alley. Cameron allowed him to place the bag into his hand. Cameron inspected the pills through the bag before opening it. He dropped the four little white pills in his hand. They looked harmless. One pill was faced upward. He could barely make out the imprint, M367, pressed on the pills. Cameron looked confused. He looked up at the guy.

"It looks like extra strength Motrin, don't it?" The guy smirked. He thought his joke was cunning.

"Man, I only got $20." Cameron pulled the twenty from his back pocket. It was the money his mom gave him for lunch. He planned to stop at a chicken joint nearby for dinner.

The guy snatched the twenty from his hand. "It's cool this time, but next time you have to pay full price."

Cameron still wasn't sure if he even wanted the pills, but he slid the pills and the little bag into his pocket. "Alright." Cameron turned to walk away.

"Ay man, but make sure you only take one. Maybe even half of one.

Any more than that would be fatal."

"A pill?"

"I'm telling you, man. I want to see you out here in a couple days. I know you'll be back. They always come back." The guy smiled. He left down the alley, away from the school.

Cameron went back to the corner behind the gym. The two coaches were still there talking. They couldn't find Mr. Chuck's keys. He couldn't drive his Charger home. Those were the keys that Cameron picked up, the ones he had in his pocket. Coach Black was going to take Mr. Chuck home. His house was only three blocks away on Clydesdale Street. Cameron knew Clydesdale Street. How hard could it be to find this ugly green and yellow house?

Cameron wanted to confront him. He wanted to tell him how miserable he had been because of him. But who was Cameron kidding? He was six foot six inches on the outside, but felt no taller than three feet on the inside. Cameron just went home. He caught the bus to the apartment he shared with his mother.

He was happy that his mother wouldn't be there. She had already told him she was going to happy hour with her new coworkers that evening after work. He could use the quiet time to decide what he would do. Maybe Mr. Chuck forgot. Maybe he would never say anything and Mr. Chuck would never say anything either. Maybe it was like people thought. Maybe he was confused and Mr. Chuck hadn't really-. Cameron couldn't even finish the thought.

He knew that he had been violated. He knew Mr. Chuck knew it was wrong because he told him not to tell. Actually, his exact words were, "People will never believe you if you say something about this. They'll think you're just a confused little boy. You don't want people calling you a liar, do you?" And Mr. Chuck was right.

It all came back to Cameron. He had tried all those years to bury the feelings, but they had all come back. He felt helpless, just like he felt the day Mr. Chuck touched him, when Mr. Chuck told him he liked it and he was confused. He didn't think it felt bad, but he knew it was wrong. Mr. Chuck knew it was wrong.

He wondered if that's why Brodrick beat him so badly. He probably did something to him, too. He probably did something to a lot of kids simply because Cameron never went through with his case. Cameron ran away. He thought he could run away from his problems but instead, he left Mr. Chuck to do the same thing he did to him to other kids. Cameron had to end the turmoil. He didn't stay and fight then, but he would stay and fight now. He would finish what Brodrick started.

Cameron took his mom's gun from the shoebox in the closet and hopped back on the bus. He wouldn't kill Mr. Chuck, he'd just confront him. He'd have to take him serious if he had a gun, Right? He could tell him to leave the school forever or he would tell everyone what he did. Cameron didn't know what he'd do, but he'd do something.

He jumped off the bus when it got to Clydesdale Street. He was grateful that the sun hadn't too long set, so he wouldn't be noticeable. He spotted the ugly green and yellow house with a car in front of it. If someone was there, Mr. Chuck would never tell the truth. Cameron went to the backdoor and waited.

The backyard was small. It was completely dark, except for the light coming from the small kitchen door window. He put his ear against the glass at the backdoor and heard Mr. Chuck walk Coach Black to the door before turning off a light. The small light above the stove was the only illumination Cameron could see in the house.

He was afraid. His heart beat fast, but he was determined to go through it. He pulled the keys from his pocket. He tried the one that looked like a house key and it turned. Cameron took a deep breath before cracking open the back door.

He heard a faint ring from a cell phone. He stood with the backdoor barely cracked and listened. He heard Mr. Chuck's voice getting lower and lower. He figured he was walking away from the back door. A door closed and Cameron could no longer hear Mr. Chuck. A light shone in the window to the right of the backdoor. Cameron could hear Mr. Chuck end his call before finally turning off the light.

It's now or never, Cameron thought to himself. He slowly pushed his way through the back door and closed it quickly behind him. He needed to put his hand on the gun in case Mr. Chuck came back.

Cameron was scared. He may never get this chance again. He would just confront Mr. Chuck, make him apologize, and he'd be done with it. Cameron set Mr. Chuck's keys on the kitchen bar, then wrapped both of his hands around the gun, just like he had seen the cops do in the movies. He had held his mom's gun before, so he felt comfortable with it, but he had never shot it. He wasn't even sure if it had bullets. He just wanted to scare Mr. Chuck in case he tried to hurt him.

Cameron heard quick footsteps, followed by a faint knock at the door. Someone was coming. He looked around and managed to slide into the kitchen pantry at the same time the front door opened. He immediately felt dumb for being there. Cameron talked himself out of confronting Mr. Chuck. As soon as he confirmed that the lady was no longer there, he was going to walk right out that back door.

He pulled his phone out of his pocket. His mom had messaged that she'd be home later than she had planned. *This is it, Cam. You have to do it now,* Cameron thought to himself. No more stalling, no more waiting. He rushed down the hallway, took a deep breath, then opened the last door.

It was dark. He couldn't see anything. He quickly found the light switch to the left of the door. He turned it on in time to see Mr. Chuck stirring in his bed. Cameron squeezed both hands around the gun again.

"Take whatever you want," Mr. Chuck sat up as soon as he saw the gun.

Cameron walked over to the bed. He towered over Mr. Chuck. Suddenly, he didn't feel so small. He felt powerful. It was the first time in his life that he had ever felt powerful.

"Take what I want?" Cameron repeated him. "I want you to apologize. I want you to apologize for what you did to me six years ago." Cameron's hands were shaking. Suddenly, the gun felt heavier.

"What did I do to you?" Mr. Chuck questioned. "Who are you?"

Before Cameron could speak, Mr. Chuck made that familiar grin. Cameron could tell that he recognized him.

"Little Cam? Is that you?"

Cameron hated that nickname. He always thought it was patronizing. He hated that grin, too. He could see it clearly through that busted lip. That grin that said he could do whatever he wanted to whomever he wanted. He could do it and get away with it. Cameron shook the gun to let him know that he was serious. "Apologize!" Cameron made his voice deeper, so Mr. Chuck would know that he meant business.

"What do you want me to say, Little Cam? Whatever I did to you, I'm sure you liked it."

Cameron jumped at the sound of a phone ringing. Mr. Chuck's phone rang on the nightstand next to his bed, next to the bottle of Motrin. "Don't you think about it," Cameron growled.

The pill bottle reminded Cameron of the pills in his pocket. Keeping the gun pointed at Mr. Chuck, Cameron pulled the pills out of his pocket. Mr. Chuck wasn't at all as apologetic as Cameron had hoped. Cameron knew that Mr. Chuck was just waiting on the chance to overtake him, to knock the gun out of his hand. That was a risk that

Cameron didn't want to make.

If Mr. Chuck was woozy, he couldn't fight him. If he was high, he might confess. Cameron might even be able to catch it on video. Embarrass Mr. Chuck the way Mr. Chuck embarrassed him.

"Take these. They'll get you to tell the truth."

Mr. Chuck laughed. He opened his hand to accept the pills. He looked at them. "Is this Motrin?" He looked back up at Cameron. "You want me to take Motrin?"

"Just take the damn pills, Mr. Chuck."

"If I take them, will you put the gun down?"

Cameron shook the gun at him again. "Take them."

"Can I just take one?"

"Take them all now!" Cameron grasped the gun with both hands again and aimed at Mr. Chuck's chest. He made sure not to get too close.

"Alright, Alright." Mr. Chuck threw all four of the pills in his mouth. Cameron watched as he took a gulp of water from the bottle on his nightstand.

"Now, what?" Mr. Chuck asked.

"Apologize. Apologize for touch…" Cameron couldn't bring himself to say it. "For molest…" Cameron took a deep breath. This was not how this was supposed to go. Mr. Chuck was supposed to say he was wrong. That he didn't mean to hurt Cameron and that he had some sick fetish that he was going to get help for. He was supposed to vow that he would never hurt another kid again. That he would maybe tell Cameron's mom that he wasn't confused. That he was a creep.

"Why should I apologize for doing something that you liked? You liked it, didn't you?"

"No, I didn't like it. I didn't like you. I was just a kid. You told everyone that I was confused."

"You were confused, Little Cam. Just like you are now."

"Adults aren't supposed to touch kids. Adults are supposed to protect-"

"Well, you're not a kid anymore, are you?" Mr. Chuck tried to stand and fell back onto the bed. "What? What did you give me?"

Cameron stepped back out of Mr. Chuck's reach. "Motrin," he stated. He was happy that the drugs were kicking in so fast. He didn't want to shoot Mr. Chuck, but he wasn't going to let him fight him either. He could see Mr. Chuck saying that he tried to rob him.

"I feel…" Mr. Chuck's voice trailed off. He fell back onto his pillow and closed his eyes.

"Mr. Chuck?" Cameron looked at him. He looked for signs of breathing. His chest wasn't moving. Cameron wanted to check his neck to see if he had a pulse, but what if Mr. Chuck was just tricking him? What if he was going to grab the gun as soon as he got close?

Cameron poked Mr. Chuck with the gun, but he didn't move. He kicked his leg to the side, but it fell back limp. He was pretty sure that Mr. Chuck was dead. The guy told him to take one pill. Is this what he meant by fatal? Mr. Chuck took four.

Cameron moved out of the house quickly. He left the same way that he came in, making sure to wipe his possible fingerprints from the bedroom door, kitchen pantry, and back door. He made it home only moments before his mom. The gun was already put away when she found him lying in his bed under the covers.

Cameron wasn't sure that Mr. Chuck was dead until the assembly at school. Cameron was supposed to be happy that Mr. Chuck wouldn't hurt anyone else anymore. That was supposed to make Cameron feel good. The guy that forced him to do inappropriate things could torment him no more. But why didn't he feel better? Why was Cameron still depressed?

What did you think? See what others thought and add your comments in our virtual library at www.cjkpublishing.com/library

Don't stop there. CJK Publishing has engaging stories for the entire family.

Greatest Hall of Fame

Inspire youth with this beginner chapter book series. Read along as the main character, Braxton, is encouraged to reach his goals by seeing the strength of historical figures. All within the Greatest Hall of Fame. Reading level: ages 7-9. Available in print, e-book and audiobook format.

Demarcus Jones and the Solar Calendar intertwines historical facts with current events. The book series helps youth understand the plight of the African Diaspora through the adventures of a pre-teen. Reading level: ages 9 – 12. Available in print, e-book and audio-book formats.

Innovative Inner G's is a variety book that celebrates Black excellence. The coloring pages, lists, games, mazes and more are fun for the entire family. Appropriate for all ages.

When tragedy occurs, everyone claims to know what happened, but there's only one truth. Each book in the 20 People's Lies Book series begins with the facts of the disaster, with multiple witnesses to follow. Do you think you can uncover the truth before time runs out? Appropriate for ages 14+

Our subscribers are a part of every new release. Join us by visiting
www.cjkpublishing.com/subscribe

#accidentmurderer

www.ingramcontent.com/pod-product-compliance
Lightning Source LLC
Chambersburg PA
CBHW020752210626
46807CB00018B/2530